LION CROSS POINT

LION CROSS POINT

MASATSUGU ONO

Translated by **ANGUS TURVILL**

TWO LINES
PRESS

Originally published as: 獅子渡り鼻 (Shishiwataribana)
© 2013 Masatsugu Ono
All rights reserved. First published in Japan by Kodansha Ltd.,
Tokyo. Publication rights for this English edition arranged through
Kodansha Ltd., Tokyo.

Translation © 2018 by Angus Turvill

Two Lines Press
582 Market Street, Suite 700, San Francisco, CA 94104
www.twolinespress.com

ISBN 978-1-931883-70-2

Library of Congress Control Number: 2017953866

Cover design by Liliana Lambriev
Cover photo © Gabriel Barathieu
Typeset by Sloane | Samuel

Printed in the United States of America

1 3 5 7 9 10 8 6 4 2

This project is supported in part by an award from
the National Endowment for the Arts.

ART WORKS.
arts.gov

I hated it. Detested it. I just wanted to get away as soon as I could.

His mother's whisper was like blades of grass, rustling, chafed by the wind. He tried to remember the expression on her face as she spoke, but he couldn't. Wanting to recall her voice more clearly, he closed his eyes, and when he did so he saw grass—dry, sad, tired. The harder he tried to remember her voice the more chafed and torn the grass became. Patches of brown began to appear. Something was eating this wind-blown tangle, eating his mother's voice. What was it? He peered deep into the green mass, and the brown patches grew. He was probably too young to realize that the pest feasting on the grass was his own longing, his yearning to remember his mother's voice. If it kept on eating, it would soon form a chrysalis, taking the place of the bud it had consumed, and then form wings in place of the flower that would have grown. And then his mother's voice, and not just her voice but her expression too, would be recovered. But, mixed with the fluids and fibers of the bug—like how a butterfly bears no resemblance to its caterpillar—both the voice and face would have become something entirely different. Soon, evening came. The faint light on the grass weakened and everything grew darker.

I hated it. Detested it.

The voice, the chafing grass, grew hoarse. Darkness and silence. And then, after what could have been a moment or could have been a day, there was brightness. Although the things on which the soft light fell were the same as ever, in fact *because* they were the same as ever, Takeru was still here, in this place that his mother hated, and his brother was not beside him. He wondered if, just as he was without his mother and brother, some of the things around him might have lost their shadows too.

But to Takeru it didn't seem like such a terrible place. The sea was close. He could hear it when he shut his eyes. The gentle sound of the waves brought him deep and restful sleep. He had grown slow to wake, slow to rise. The village was on a narrow stretch of land between a coastal inlet and its surrounding hills. He had come here, to his mother's birthplace, to spend the summer vacation with Mitsuko. He didn't know what the connection was between Mitsuko and his mother. They could have been aunt and niece, or cousins of very different ages, or perhaps more distant relations. Regardless,

4

Mitsuko was of an age at which she could easily have been taken for ten-year-old Takeru's grandmother. She was a small, cheerful, energetic person, her back slightly hunched, her waist and shoulders thick-set. Short dense hair hemmed her narrow forehead. It was dyed black, but showed white at her temples. Her face was always either serious or smiling. Looking at Mitsuko, Takeru realized that his mother's expression was probably always somewhere in between. But in the broad range between a serious, brooding look and a smile, Takeru could find nothing to hold on to. So he was never able to build an image, and his mother's face slipped like smoke between the fingers of his memory.

"I'm only here for the summer, right?"

"That what ya been told?" replied Mitsuko.

Takeru didn't answer.

"First I heard of it," said Mitsuko. "Who said that?"

Then, looking deep into Takeru's eyes, she asked, "You wanna go home? Back to your ma?"

Again, Takeru said nothing.

Mitsuko smiled.

"If ya wanna stay, you can, long as you like."

Mitsuko always gave Takeru a way out. If he didn't answer a question he'd feel stranded in a dark hole—but then she'd gently open a door. Even when he wanted to speak, he wasn't good at it; and there were some things he didn't know if he could speak about at all. For a child like him, a woman like Mitsuko was bound to be a comfort. And everybody here was kind, not just her. Not that he'd met that many people.

That day, as he woke from a nap, he had the vague feeling that Bunji was in the room. He wondered why Bunji didn't leave the area. It couldn't simply be because people here were kind. Perhaps these thoughts came to him because he had just been dreaming about his brother. In the dream his brother had been asleep—face down, one cheek pressed against a tatami mat, his mouth squashed and pouting like a fish's, a strand of drool hanging from his lip. They were in the apartment in Akeroma where they had lived with their mother, though she had almost always been away. The cries of cicadas poured in through the open window, a shower of sound that smothered all other noise, yet seemed to intensify the smell of rotting garbage that clung to the air. Unless the garbage was in the apartment, the smell must have come in through the window as well. Perhaps the flapping of agitated crows fanned it in. The window had no curtains and the fierce afternoon sun burned down on the tatami where his brother lay. From time to time his brother groaned. He tossed and turned. It was as though when asleep, yes, only when asleep, Takeru's brother too might have felt troubled. Was that true? It was Takeru who was troubled, desperate at the thought of his brother waking up his usual self. No, he wasn't. He was used to it. Was that true? You couldn't get inside someone else's sleep, so even if there was a maelstrom in his brother's head, he wouldn't be able to witness it. But there'd be even less chance of finding out once his brother was awake, wouldn't there? His brother wouldn't reply, couldn't reply.

Of course, Takeru knew perfectly well that what he was doing wouldn't get him inside his brother's mind. Yet in the depths of sleep his brother looked so defenseless (but against what, whom?), submissive (but to what, whom?), and exposed (but to what, whom?). At the same time his little body was like impenetrable armor. It protected his mind, hidden away within. It was closed—firmly and stubbornly. As though tempted by the very strangeness of it, Takeru lowered his clenched fist to his brother's face. One cheek was flat against the floor. The other bulged upward, and Takeru pushed his fist gently against it. He suddenly increased the pressure and, thinking this might be a way to break through the armor, rotated his fist left and right. Then from behind his ears, from the depths of the dream—no, from somewhere quite unknown—he heard that voice, that bizarre, high-pitched, strangled voice:

Don't! Don't do that!

It was no longer his brother who turned in his sleep, but Takeru. He woke up.

He knew the person whose voice it was would be there when he opened his eyes. He was always there. Bunji. His face, with its little eyes and nose, forming its usual expression—a smile? confusion?—looking down

7

at Takeru. Or perhaps Bunji wasn't looking at Takeru. To Takeru, those eyes seemed to look inward, inside Bunji himself. But how can somebody's eyes, that only ever point outward, look within?

"Like this."

That's what old Tsuru in the village would have said. Tsuru was always sitting at the bus stop at the intersection, where the main coastal road from the north meets a local road that leads to another village on an inlet to the east. Veins stood out on his palms like worms, and in the warmth of one of those palms he kept his fake eye. He liked to roll it around and then put it, backward, into his left eye socket. Takeru couldn't get used to it. He stiffened with disgust every time Tsuru did it. Tsuru would look at Takeru and smile—a faint slit appearing between his thin, wrinkled lips.

Takeru never asked Tsuru what he could see with the eye in backward. It seemed to Takeru that at the back of Tsuru's empty eye socket, at the back of his mouth too, there would be an expanse of terrifying darkness.

"Everyone's eyes're like this when they sleep," Tsuru said. "They roll right back."

Takeru didn't know if that was true or not. But he remembered seeing white between his sleeping brother's eyelids. Perhaps his own eyes would look the same if he could see himself asleep.

"When we dream I figure we see a landscape inside ourselves," said Tsuru.

If that was the case, then what about Bunji? He looked like he was dreaming even when he was awake. What did those eyes of his show him? An always unfamiliar scene of desolation? No. Takeru imagined it to be a land of green grass and trees, of brightly colored flowers, of clear water. In fact, Takeru could see it. It was a warm place, but cool in the morning and evening even on the hottest days, so you had to cover up at night. It was a land between green mountains and dark blue sea, which meant it was here. Right here. This place that his mother hated, detested.

When, in his dream about the apartment in Akeroma, Takeru heard the alarm in Bunji's voice, he lifted his fist off of his brother's cheek. Bunji's tone suggested an intimacy with Takeru and his brother, so Takeru felt, more than ever, like he had known Bunji for a long time. But he couldn't have. The first time Takeru saw Bunji was at the airport, on the day he arrived here.

Mitsuko had come all the way to Tokyo to pick him up and bring him to his mother's old village by the sea. She wasn't used to trains, and they had to transfer several times on the way from Akeroma to the Tokyo airport. She kept checking with the station staff, or anybody else around, to make sure that she and Takeru weren't getting on the wrong train. They got to the airport two hours before their flight. Although there was plenty of time, Mitsuko was all flustered, rushing to buy presents for people back home. In the end she bought so many that she couldn't carry them, and had to ask the shop to ship some of them for her. But she seemed embarrassed as she spoke to the shopgirl. She was trying to speak Tokyo Japanese, which wasn't natural for her at all.

She turned to Takeru as she was filling in her address and muttered, "Oh dear, I've used a whole year's spendin' money."

"Will you be paying with cash or a card, Madam?"

"Card?" Mitsuko frowned, as though a credit card might carry a curse. "No! Oh no!" she said, waving a hand in front of her face. "Cash!"

Mitsuko looked very tense as she paid. She spoke to Takeru in a hurried whisper, but he didn't really understand what she was saying:

"A credit card takes money straight out your 'count, don't it? What if it takes out t'much and you don't realize it? I don't like things like that…"

Unfortunately, Mitsuko's intended whisper was loud enough for the pretty, young shop assistant to hear. Takeru saw the girl put her hand to her mouth and snicker. He felt awkward. He didn't want to look at either Mitsuko or the girl, so he kept his eyes on the floor.

"Restaurants're too expensive," sighed Mitsuko, having spent so much money on gifts. "Save, save, save," she muttered as she made her way to a food stall, where she bought some lunch boxes and tea. The high-ceilinged lobby was lined with seating. They chose a place and settled down to eat.

"Taste good, don't it, Takeru."

Mitsuko sounded as though she really meant it, and maybe that made it taste good to Takeru too.

It wasn't yet the peak summer vacation period, so their flight just before 2 p.m. had quite a few empty seats. Most of the other passengers were businessmen in white button-down shirts. Across the aisle from Takeru was a middle-aged man with his shoes off, reading a newspaper. There were a few women and children on the plane as well, no doubt traveling early to spend the *bon* holidays with grandparents. A boy of about Takeru's age was being told off by his mother for not sharing his manga book or game console with his little brother. Mitsuko fell asleep shortly after takeoff. Takeru looked at the side of her face. He'd been told that he'd met her when he was small, but he couldn't remember. Takeru grew sleepy too. When he opened his eyes again Mitsuko was awake.

"What's the matter?" asked Mitsuko, feeling Takeru's eyes on her.

No, he had no memory of her at all.

But the person at the airport seemed familiar right away. Takeru and Mitsuko had picked up their luggage and were walking through the arrivals gate. The person was sitting on a bench by the glass wall of the lobby, thin and frail. Because he was sitting down, it was difficult to be sure of how tall he was, but he struck Takeru as very short, probably no taller than Takeru himself.

What was most remarkable was his face. It was like a

child's, yet at the same time like that of someone very old. But then it was neither. A mysterious face, as though immaturity and the decrepitude of age had fused together in a fight for center ground. Takeru had no idea how old the person was, but there was no doubt he was male. He couldn't tell whether the person was looking at him or not. Somehow he reminded Takeru of the old woman who'd always been kind to him at the supermarket in Akeroma. Of course, they couldn't be the same person.

"Hii-chan!" Mitsuko shouted, waving her arm. "O'er here!"

But she wasn't calling to the person on the bench; she was calling to a man farther down the arrivals hall. He hurried cheerfully toward them. He was small and wore a Hawks baseball cap.

"You're late," said Hii-chan. His face was ruddy, and he had a very large nose. His long white eyebrows hung down to his dark, mischievous, sparkling eyes.

"Your flight was takin' so long I went t'see if there was any news 'bout a crash on TV," he said, pointing to the large screen at the other end of the hall.

"Don't be silly," laughed Mitsuko. "We got lots to carry so give us a hand. I got ya a present, by the way."

Hii-chan took her bag of presents. It was so full of candy boxes it was beginning to tear.

"Whoa! So many gifts!" he said, with an exaggerated show of surprise. "Are you a millionaire now?"

He turned to Takeru.

"Welcome!" he said kindly. "Glad t'meet ya."

Takeru took off his FC Barcelona cap and bobbed his head. His bangs were sticking to his forehead with sweat. Hii-chan frowned at the length of Takeru's hair.

"What's all that for? Don't it get in the way? You should get yourself a haircut like me, kid!"

Hii-chan took off his cap with one hand and rubbed his shaved scalp with the other. He smiled, a silver tooth glinting in his mouth.

Neither Hii-chan nor Mitsuko looked even once at the person on the bench, and they didn't seem to notice Takeru stealing glances in his direction.

Hii-chan had parked in the lot in front of the airport. Takeru followed him and Mitsuko out of the lobby and across the road. He then stopped and turned around. He could see the man through the shiny blue plate glass, his head oddly large against his slight frame, his back stooped. The man wasn't looking in his direction, so that was all that Takeru could make out. He turned away and hurried after Mitsuko.

Takeru was astonished to see the man again the next day, after his first night at Mitsuko's house. When he got up Mitsuko was placing a bowl of rice on the family altar, as she did first thing every morning.

"Come here, Takeru," she said. "Look, these're your relatives. Tell 'em you've come home, and ask 'em to look after ya."

Takeru pressed his palms together in front of the altar and did as he was told. "I've come home. Please look after me."

Then he pointed to the small wooden altar drum. "Can I hit that?" he asked.

"Sure," said Mitsuko, handing him a stick.

He tapped the drum and began to chant: "Dummy number dummy number…"—his approximation of a prayer to the Amida Buddha.

Mitsuko laughed.

"Look!" she said. "My old man's enjoyin' that!"

On the altar were some small framed photographs. One showed a man of about sixty-five in a suit—Mitsuko's late husband, Yoshio. He was definitely smiling. Takeru's tapping quickened and his voice grew louder. He looked carefully at the other photos to see if anyone else was smiling. That was when he noticed. The oldest photo on the altar was so faded that you could hardly even call it black and white. He stretched up to take a better look. In the photo, a group of about ten adults and children were gathered around a bald hermit-like old man with a long goatee, who was sitting on the veranda of an old-fashioned house. In the foreground were a wicker bamboo bowl, some chickens, and a piglet. Takeru's eye was caught by a woman standing near the frame, farthest away from the old man. She was staring out of the picture with a suspicious frown. Takeru's dubious mantra stopped. The drum fell silent.

"Who's this, Mitsuko?" he said.

"Which one?" she asked, coming closer to the altar. She picked up the photo and held it out to Takeru.

"The boy standing in front of that woman…"

"Ah…that's her son, Bunji."

The shaven-headed boy in the picture was just a child. But Takeru felt sure it was him—the man he'd seen at the airport, the man he somehow felt he already knew. Takeru was about to say so to Mitsuko, but he didn't. The boy in the picture was looking down—perhaps he was nervous about the piglet whose nose was so close to his foot that it might almost have been eating it. Takeru couldn't see enough to judge whether his features were definitely those of the face he'd seen yesterday—the strange face that could have belonged either to a young child or an old man. And besides, Mitsuko had suddenly started talking, excited, as though she'd noticed something important in the picture that she'd never seen before.

"Oh, look! Can ya see the kid Bunji's ma's holdin'? That's Bunji's little brother—Takeshi. A lot like your name."

"Well, yeah," said Takeru, "but it's not the same. I'm Takeru, not Takeshi."

"Of course. But at first we all thought you were called Takeshi. I can't 'member why we thought that, but everyone said your ma must've named ya after this Takeshi in the photo. He was a cousin of your ma's grandpa—a very clever boy who got into the Naval Officers' School. So we thought your ma, Wakako, named ya after him. But really, I don't suppose your ma would've even known 'bout him."

Mitsuko's tone then changed—it was as if she was saying something she didn't really want to. She wouldn't have been good at telling lies.

"We didn't even know your ma had a child 'til years after ya were born. And for a long time we all thought your name was Takeshi. Your ma never came home for Bon or the New Year. Didn't even send a New Year's card. We had no idea what she was doin' with her life. We didn't even know if she was alive. We had no word at all and it upset us…but she always was that kind of girl."

Had his mother not told people in the village about his brother? That's what Takeru wanted to ask, but his mouth said something different. He pointed at the boy in its mother's arms and the boy standing in front of her:

"What happened to them? Are they still alive?"

"They died a long, long time ago. If they were alive today, they'd be over a hundred. I never knew either of 'em."

Something inside Takeru wanted to block out the sound of her voice, but it was powerless, so he heard everything she said.

"Bunji died when he was very young—just a child. Takeshi was in the Navy durin' the war. Then with the American 'cupation there were restrictions on jobs for officers out of the military, so he came back here and set up a fishin' business. When the restrictions were lifted he was 'lected a councilman. But then, shortly after, he drowned at sea. It seems like such a waste that he died like that, after he made it through the war."

She sighed, but didn't say any more. *Two brothers—like you.* That would have been an obvious thing to say, thought Takeru. But of course she didn't say it. She was kind. She'd taken him in, and she never cornered him. She wouldn't say something like that.

Takeru didn't feel confident to answer questions about his brother, but he always expected to be asked. But neither Mitsuko nor anyone else he met in the village ever mentioned him. They occasionally brought up his mother, but never his brother. It was strange. It was almost as if he'd never had a brother. Perhaps he hadn't. Was that the truth of the matter? He wished it was.

Takeru met Saki Kawano a couple of days later. Mitsuko had gone out to a local Welfare and Children's Committee meeting and Takeru was watching television alone when he heard a child's voice:

"Mitsuko!"

He stood up, went to the kitchen, opened the back door, and found a girl standing outside. Her black hair was straight, her bangs cut at right angles above her neat eyebrows. She had large long-lashed eyes that curved down slightly toward her cheekbones. It was a regular southern face. He knew right away that she was from the house next door—he'd caught sight of her a couple of times coming or going. Seeing her up close for the first time, he noticed her long thin limbs. She was slightly taller than he was. She had probably seen him before as well. Her big sparkling eyes stared at him more in friendly curiosity than surprise.

"Who're you?" she asked.

"Takeru Tamura," he said.

"I'm Saki," she said. "Saki Kawano. Where're you from?"

"Tokyo…" said Takeru vaguely.

"What grade?"

"Fourth."

"I'm in second."

Knowing he was two years older than her, Takeru now felt bolder.

"So what do you want?" he said.

For a moment Saki looked surprised. Takeru thought maybe he'd sounded conceited. Her hands shot out. They held a small cooking pot.

"Please thank Mitsuko for us," she said. "It was delicious."

Takeru took the pot and Saki opened the door to leave. Then, with her hand still on the doorknob, she turned around as though something had just occurred to her. She looked very serious.

"Can ya play tomorrow?" she said.

Before Takeru had time to nod, the door slammed shut.

Through the door he could hear the girl running on the white gravel outside the house. It seemed like a happy sound.

Mitsuko came home shortly afterward. She picked up the pot from the table.

"Saki bring this back?" she asked.

She ran her finger around the rim of the pot.

"She always brings things back so clean," she said, as though to herself. "I suppose she's the one that washes 'em. She's a good girl."

Saki and her father lived in the two-story house next door, beyond a small field of cucumbers and onions. According to Mitsuko, they'd moved in about four years ago when the house was new. Because there was no woman in their house, Mitsuko took over food whenever she could—*nikujaga*, curry, boiled fish, sashimi.

Saki's father, Tatsuya, had worked at Kawase Fisheries, one of the biggest fisheries in the area, based in a village that had once been the administrative hub of the district. But he had given up that job and bought the house in Takanoura. He had also bought a small second-hand boat and started fishing on his own, but the boat was always tied up at the quay now. Neither Mitsuko nor anybody else in Takanoura knew what he lived on. Some people said he made money playing pachinko. That was the opinion of Chikara Goto, a fisherman friend of Mitsuko's late husband, who sometimes stopped by to bring her fish. The evidence he gave to support his theory was how often he spotted Tatsuya's car in the parking lot of one of the pachinko parlors on the main road in "town" (as the local people called the built-up area beyond the hill).

"He goes so often he's gotta be livin' off it," said Chikara smugly.

"So how come you ain't livin' off it, Chika?" asked Mitsuko.

She looked entirely earnest, without a hint of malice or hidden motive. Chikara smiled awkwardly. His chubby face, always red and beading with sweat, grew even redder.

Tatsuya would sometimes come to the door when Mitsuko took food to the house. He was tall and thin, with a slight stoop. His hair was always unkempt, his face unshaven, his eyes bloodshot and puffy. It was hard to believe those eyes could belong to the father of a girl whose eyes were so big and clear. When he opened the door it always looked as though he'd just been asleep. He'd appear in a crumpled T-shirt and shorts or track pants that he'd obviously just put on. He often stank of cheap liquor.

Mitsuko couldn't help but mutter under her breath at the sight of him. Being on the local Welfare and Children's Committee, she felt she should express her concerns clearly. But she was disarmed by Tatsuya's affable, slightly sad, smile.

"Thank ya," he'd say, bowing his head. "You're always so kind."

"No bother," she'd say. "We're neighbors, after all. We've gotta look after each other." What else could she say?

"And thanks for that stew you gave us t'other day— Saki really loved it. 'Scrumptious,' she said. She ended up eatin' my helpin' too."

His back would hunch up when he spoke this way, and he'd sound so apologetic that the kindhearted Mitsuko found herself unable to say anything critical.

His words suggested that he didn't leave his daughter to eat on her own. That at least was something. Before setting off from her house with a pan or tray, Mitsuko always resolved to deliver one or two harsh truths when she arrived. But when leaving his house she'd find herself cheerfully saying things like: "Okay! I'll have t'make more next time so there's enough for you too!" It was as if, unable to confront him, she'd decide that both Tatsuya and she herself would benefit from a bit of positivity. Then she'd walk home, her head cocked to one side, wondering what had happened.

The fact that nobody ever saw Tatsuya working didn't mean that the household was broken or degenerate. There was no screaming or shouting to be heard, no sounds of things smashing, no endless, heart-wrenching crying. In fact, the house was rather quiet. If a window was open, the sound of the TV came out—sports highlights, or laughter from a variety show—blending with the cries of the insects. Occasionally, Mitsuko worried that the TV was on too late, but it didn't happen often. Sometimes Tatsuya put out the wash—both his and his daughter's clothes—too late in the day to dry, but it nearly always appeared at some point during the day. Peering inside through the front or back door there were no signs that the house was a mess. Mitsuko felt sorry for Saki, having no mother, but the girl didn't look unhappy.

"It reminds me of when your ma was little," Mitsuko said one day out of the blue. Takeru couldn't imagine his mother as a child.

Once she saw that Takeru and Saki had become friends it became easier for Mitsuko to invite Saki over for a meal. "Dad says it's okay," Saki would say when she arrived, without Mitsuko having to ask whether she had permission. Before long she was a regular visitor, coming over to have dinner or a snack with Takeru.

Mitsuko's house had a wide veranda that faced south, where Mitsuko placed a folding table for them. She lit a mosquito coil and when Takeru complained about the heat, she brought out an electric fan, the cord stretching from inside. The breeze from the fan dispersed the smoke from the mosquito coil, but at the same time made it difficult for the light, black insects to get close to the bodies at the table. The mosquitoes hung in the air, impotent yet threatening. It was difficult for thoughts to take shape when they were hovering there, hard for sentences to fall into place. Maybe only simple things could be said—like what Takeru said now:

"Showa."

Mitsuko laughed.

"What's so funny?" he said.

"You mean the fan and coil make ya think of the Showa Period? What do *you* know about the Showa Period? It ended years ago." she said.

Takeru pouted, his tight lips pressed forward like a mosquito's proboscis. Then he heard a voice. Or thought he heard a voice.

Don't! Don't talk about things you don't know.

Takeru glanced across the table at Saki. Her face was turned in the direction from which the voice had come. Takeru turned to gaze the same way. He could see Saki's house beyond the vegetable field, slightly obstructed by the kurogane holly tree that grew at the edge of Mitsuko's garden. Beside the tree stood Bunji. His back was tight against its pale trunk. Maybe he thought he was hidden. Maybe he thought he'd become part of the tree. His hands were over his mouth, as if he'd said something he shouldn't have, and his shoulders were hitching up and down. He looked comical. Takeru imagined Bunji criticizing himself, his voice screeching in time with the jolting of his shoulders: *Don't! Don't poke your nose into other people's business!*

Takeru felt certain that Saki had also noticed Bunji. He watched her as she turned back to the table.

"Dad hasn't taken the clothes in," she said. "I'll have t'go and take 'em in soon."

"Yeah," said Mitsuko. "But you won't be able t'reach. I'll take it in for ya later, don't worry 'bout it."

Takeru looked at the tree again. Bunji wasn't there anymore. But he could see him plodding along the narrow concrete road between the fields that led north to the seawall. He was bent forward, as though carrying something heavy on his back. Against his small thin body Bunji's hands looked strangely large, dangling weakly by his thighs. Beyond him were hills. A hill to the west, one of the two that formed the bay, was beginning to cast a purple shadow over the village, a sign that night was not far off. A half-transparent moon hung in the sky. From time to time there was the noise of a vehicle on the bay road, which had been straightened during the coastal protection program. The cicadas were as loud as ever. The cries of black hawks fell from the sky like quoits, hoops of sound thrown down toward trees and telephone poles. The hawks themselves, descending more swiftly than their cries, settled here and there on the poles, folded their scruffy wings, and stared fixedly toward something more distant than tomorrow.

Takeru thought of Bunji's eyes and wondered if they could see this scenery. Tottering along the road Bunji looked spurned by the world outside himself, by this land. But from what Mitsuko had said, Bunji had died without ever leaving, without ever going beyond the boundaries of the green hills and dark blue sea. So, how could it be that there was no place for him here, where he'd been born and lived his whole life? His eyes looked as though they couldn't see what was in front of him, as if—though no one else was there to see it either—the scene hid itself from him, refused to let him see it. So his vision couldn't expand outward, and had no alternative but to go inward. But what was there inside? Any memories that might rise up from the dark depths inside him would be memories of this land between the green hills and dark blue sea, this land that was now sinking into the depths of night. There was nothing else inside him but the very scenery that so stubbornly refused to accept him. Even if he'd tried to remember any other landscape he wouldn't have been able to—there was nowhere else he knew. And he couldn't have created fake memories for himself. Mitsuko said he hadn't been bright, hadn't gone to school. If you've got nowhere to go in reality, then at least you'd want your mind to take you somewhere. But if you don't understand what people say, if you can't read or write, how could you imagine another world?

Rejected both from within and without, where was Bunji trying to go? Was he unable to go anywhere, and thus had no choice but to remain here? The expression of Bunji's eye was stuck fast in the surface of its lens. Clear but at the same time blurred. It was just the same as… whom? Takeru must have known from the start. But he would only realize later that every time a word for that person, or an image of them, came into his mind, he tried to get rid of it immediately, as though crumpling up a yellowing scrap of paper on which it had appeared. Takeru seemed to have been given the task of seeing Bunji, even when everyone else's sight rejected him. Who or what had imposed this duty on him? This place, of course. There was no other possibility. In which case, the place was not necessarily ignoring Bunji, not necessarily rejecting him entirely. Didn't that make sense? If Takeru could see Bunji so clearly, that meant that the landscape—everything alive and dead from which the landscape was formed—was, to at least a very small degree, yielding to Bunji, yielding something of the outline and density of existence, and so was preventing, if only just, his complete disappearance. Doesn't that make sense? Yes. It's a reasonable idea. Bunji faded into the dusk, and then Takeru saw his brother in the darkness instead, asleep on his stomach, his face flat against the tatami mat. The top half of his body was naked, and an ant was crawling up his thin arm. Before any other ants could appear, Takeru opened his eyes. It was only then that he realized they'd been closed.

Takeru had been dreaming of his sleeping brother again, and again it was Bunji's voice that brought him up from the depths of the dream, so when he opened his eyes he wouldn't have been surprised to see Bunji's face. But it was actually Saki who'd woken him, coming through the back door of Mitsuko's house.

"Oh…Saki," Takeru said, rubbing his eyes. "What's up?"

"You promised to play today," said Saki.

"Oh, I'm sorry!"

Saki smirked.

"What?" Takeru asked.

"Your cheek looks funny. Like it's been pressed against a tatami mat."

"I was fast asleep," said Takeru, not really feeling like he had been.

"And ya got drool down your chin."

"Do I?" he said, quickly wiping his mouth and chin with his hand.

He remembered that Mitsuko had gone out, leaving a five-hundred-yen coin on the table so that he and Saki could buy some drinks or ice cream. His mother had often left money for him like that when she was busy, back in Akeroma. But that hadn't been for treats—it had been for meals.

Gripping the coin tight in one hand, Takeru took his FC Barcelona cap from the back of the chair and hurried out after Saki. Bunji shouted from behind, as though pushing him forward.

Get ice cream. Enough for two—for you and your big brother!

Takeru stopped and looked around. *That's nasty*, he muttered. Did Bunji hear? Even if he had, he wouldn't have understood what Takeru meant. But he must have sensed Takeru's discomfort, because he put one of his big hands over his mouth, and the other went to the top of his head. *I want to vanish*, the gesture seemed to say. But he didn't have to vanish. Takeru pulled down the brim of his cap. That always made things he didn't want to see disappear.

Takeru and Saki went out to the road along the seawall, and soon reached the main highway that ran north-south through Takanoura. There was a good breeze where the roads met, and Takeru thought of old Tsuru holding his glass eye up to the sun. "This spot has the best light in the village," he had mumbled, his jaw jerking. In the mornings old people could often be seen chatting at the bus stop. They'd be there in the late afternoons too, or they'd go to the seawall before the warmth of the day faded. Whenever he walked past, Takeru was nervous that he might see Tsuru again, but today the sun was still hot and there was nobody around. Now and then a car passed, disturbing the hot, heavy, clinging air. No. What stirred was time, which had been drowsing and had forgotten to move on.

They turned south along the highway and went to the Shudo Gas Station, which had a vending machine—the closest one to Mitsuko's house. No vehicles were filling up or being washed. There were four or five small cars for sale along the retaining wall on the north side of the station, with prices displayed on their windshields. In the shade against the southern wall were three men as always. Well, they always seemed to be hanging around and chatting when Takeru came by. Not entirely unlike used cars that could find no buyers, they were essential to the way the gas station looked—another part of the scenery his mother hated, detested.

The young man in oil company overalls was Oil Toshi, the heir to the family gas station. He had drooping eyes and buck teeth. Long, dyed-blond hair protruded from his cap. Next to him was a man in a large straw hat, white running shirt, Bermuda shorts, and New Balance sneakers on his bare feet. Takeru knew him well. He was the man in the Hawks baseball cap who'd come to the airport to meet him and Mitsuko. He'd been in elementary school with Yoshio, Mitsuko's husband. He often dropped by Mitsuko's house, and had recently brought over a watermelon. Takeru noticed again the long white eyebrows that hung like willow down to his twinkling, mischievous eyes. Looking now at his large nose and eyes, Takeru realized what the man reminded him of. No question: a proboscis monkey. Takeru didn't know the man's real name, and like everybody else in the village, called him Hii-chan. In front of the other two was a middle-aged man in a navy T-shirt, tracksuit pants, and white rubber boots. He was tall and well-built, with gleaming eyes. He looked rather like an eagle. Takeru had asked Mitsuko who he was, but he couldn't remember what she'd said.

"Hey! Takeru and Saki!" said Hii-chan. "What're you two up to?"

The man in white boots glanced at Takeru.

"Where'd the boy come from?" he asked Hii-chan.

"I told ya 'fore. He's stayin' with Mitsuko. Wakako Tobitaka's son."

"Her name's not Tobitaka. It's Tamura," said Takeru. He could feel sweat rolling down his face.

"Sorry, Takeru!" said Hii-chan. "Your ma was a Tobitaka 'fore she married—that's how I 'member her."

"Wakako's son?" muttered the man in the white boots, his eyes curious.

For some reason Takeru felt a kind of hostility toward him. He kept his gaze on the ground, scared of catching the man's eye. At his feet was a dark patch on the concrete. It seemed to stick like glue to the soles of his shoes, not letting him move. It wasn't oil, though. It was his shadow.

"He's here for the summer," said Oil Toshi, coming to Takeru's rescue. "Third grade, ain't ya?"

"He's a fourth grader. Isn't that right, Takeru?" Saki said.

"*Isn't that right*," said Toshi, imitating her. "You sound like a girl from Tokyo!"

Saki smiled, embarrassed.

"Anyway, Saki," Toshi continued, "it's good that you're friends with Takeru. There ain't that many kids your age at school, are there? They put the grades together for classes, right? Won't be long 'til they close the school completely."

"We ain't the same age," Saki corrected him. "I told you 'fore—Takeru's a fourth grader. I'm in second grade."

"Oh, sorry," said Toshi. "You're so tall, nobody'd think ya were in second grade."

"Wakako's son…" said the man in white boots again.

The man's boots weren't, in fact, white. They were streaked with brown dirt. Takeru was still looking down, his gaze now fixed on the man's boots, white but not white. He didn't miss the momentary wince in the man's eyes, though. He didn't see it, but he knew it was there.

"Wakako back too?" the man asked Hii-chan. Then he turned to Takeru, and asked him as well. "You come back with your ma?"

Takeru stared at his shadow on the concrete. He was like the hand of a stopped clock. That's what he felt.

"She comin' later? Is Wakako…is your ma comin' for ya later?"

Takeru was silent. He could feel Saki's worried gaze on his cheek, tickling like an insect, like an ant crawling on his skin. He remembered a couple of ants crossing his brother's cheek. Maybe there were some tasty crumbs around his mouth. Just as Takeru hated being asked about his brother, he hated people talking about his mother too. He hated it even more when they were people he didn't know well. He pulled the brim of his cap down over his eyes so that he couldn't hear.

He wouldn't even have heard Bunji whispering in his ear: *It's okay. It's okay. Don't worry!*

"He don't look much like Wakako," said the man in dirty white boots to Hii-chan.

"Suppose he look more like his dad," said Hii-chan.

The coin in Takeru's hand seemed to have melted away in the sweat and heat of his clenched fist. He heard the man go on.

"I was in elementary school with your ma. Two years above her."

The man wasn't smiling (though Takeru had his eyes on the ground and his cap pulled down so didn't really know that he wasn't smiling), but his voice was friendly, so it felt as though he was smiling. The man was about to ask another question, but seeing the expression on Hii-chan's face he changed his mind. Instead he said:

"Tell your ma Ken Shiomi says 'ello. Say my name and she'll know right away."

Takeru forced himself to nod—it was like swallowing medicine. He wanted to cry. He couldn't feel the coin in his palm. It had melted away… Had he lost it somehow? That's why I want to cry, he told himself, fighting back the tears. He pulled his cap down lower still so nobody would see his face. His vision blurred as sweat dripped relentlessly into his eyes. Saki's gaze was itching on his face.

Though he could see nothing, *because* he could see nothing, he saw ants crawling up from somewhere, crawling around his brother's cheek, arms, shoulders, calves. He didn't know why he saw it. He knew, but he didn't know.

"So what can we do for ya?" Oil Toshi said kindly, leaning in close to Takeru. "You come on an errand?"

At last Takeru managed to speak.

"Um...have you got any ice cream?"

He didn't know why he said it. He knew the vending machine only sold drinks. As the words struggled from his mouth he held out his clenched hand and opened it.

And? The flesh of his palm was glistening with sweat. There was nothing else on it but sunlight. The coin had really melted away. But there was no stickiness there, like when ice cream melts. The tears on his cheeks were sticky though. Perhaps that's why the ants were gathering.

"Ice cream?" said Oil Toshi. "We don't sell ice cream..."

He pretended not to notice Takeru's empty palm. He'd seen the confusion it had brought to the boy's face.

"We got drinks," he said, pointing to the vending machine beside the office door.

"Where'd the money go?" Saki whispered in his ear, mystified.

Still hidden by his cap, Takeru blinked and blinked again. He narrowed his eyes and opened them wide, but the coin that had vanished from his palm did not reappear. He tried pushing up the brim of his cap a little, but that changed nothing. The five-hundred-yen coin had disappeared without a trace. He quietly lifted his palm to his mouth and licked. It was salty, but he thought he also noticed a metallic taste.

"What ya havin'?"

Takeru looked up. Ken was standing at the vending machine. He'd already inserted some coins from his pocket, and was poised to push a button.

"Feelin' flush, Ken?" said Hii-chan, laughing.

He turned to Takeru and Saki.

"Have whatever ya want. Just tell 'im!"

Toshi nodded.

"Go on," he said. "Have somethin'. He says it's on 'im, so you might as well."

It's okay. It's okay. Let him!

Hearing Bunji's voice, Takeru turned around, but Bunji wasn't to be seen.

Takeru said nothing.

"'kay," said Toshi. "If you prefer ice cream…"

"Iced coffee for me, Ken!" shouted Hii-chan.

A can clunked down into the delivery compartment.

"I've gone and pressed it!" Ken fretted.

He leaned down and took the coffee from the bottom of the machine. Forcing a smile, he passed the ice-cold can to Hii-chan.

"You said 'iced coffee' so I pressed the button. Didn't mean to."

"I'll put it back in the machine if ya want," said Toshi, giving Hii-chan an exaggerated wink.

"Don't worry 'bout it," said Ken, with a wave of his hand. "It's just a can of coffee after all…"

"In that case, I'll take it. Thanks!" said Hii-chan with a broad smile, his silver tooth glinting. He opened the coffee and took a sip. "Beautiful—nice and cold. Cheers!"

"You must be hot standin' there," said Ken, putting his hand against Takeru's back. "You're covered in sweat. Come over here." He led Takeru into the shade.

"You really want an ice cream?" he asked.

Takeru didn't answer, so Ken asked Saki.

"How 'bout you, Saki? Want t'come get one? I'm on my way to town now."

"But, um," mumbled Saki, glancing worriedly across at Takeru.

"That's a good idea," said Hii-chan cheerfully. "It'll be borin' for you two 'round here all day. Let Ken take ya into town."

"But," said Saki, "I'll have to tell my dad."

Ken looked amused.

"Old Tatsuya wouldn't say no, as long as you're with me! He ever said no to me takin' you anywhere 'fore?"

Saki thought for a while.

"No, Ken," she said, sounding reassured.

"See?" Ken said triumphantly.

"I'll let Mitsuko know they've gone to town with ya," said Toshi.

"Good. Thanks," Ken said.

"Don't come back too late," said Hii-chan. "Mitsuko'll be annoyed if they're late for dinner."

"Course!" said Ken, smiling.

His dark gray car was parked in the shade. He opened the rear passenger door and Saki climbed right in, as though she did it all the time.

"Uh! It's boilin'!" she yelped.

"Hang on…" said Ken. "I'll put the air-conditionin' on."

He climbed in and turned on the engine. Then he leaned over, opened the front passenger door, and beckoned to Takeru.

"Hop in!"

Takeru hesitated, but Bunji gave him a push from behind. Or maybe it was Hii-chan.

It's okay. It's okay. Get in!

After they'd been driving for a while, Saki leaned forward between the driver and passenger seats. "Ken?" she said. "When're we gonna go?"

"Where?" said Ken, puzzled. "To town? We're goin' right now."

"No!" Saki said, pouting. "Dolphin Village, of course! You said you'd take me!"

"Oh, that's what you're talkin' 'bout," he said, nodding.

"Is that the place where you can swim with dolphins?" asked Takeru, turning to Saki.

"Yes," said Saki. "You heard of it?"

"It must be famous all 'cross the country!" said Ken.

Takeru shook his head.

"I heard about it from Hii-chan," he said.

It had taken a good two hours to get from the airport to Takanoura, even on the newly built highway. On the way, Hii-chan told Takeru about Dolphin Village—a marine-life amusement park that had opened a few years before. It was just down the coast in Inonome, an area of jagged bays and inlets. Hii-chan had been there the year before with his grandchildren when they came down from Kanagawa for a visit. They had all really enjoyed it.

"Want t'go, Takeru?" Hii-chan said. "I'll take you if ya like."

"What sort of place is it?" asked Takeru. "Is it a kind of aquarium?"

"Ain't no fish there," said Hii-chan. "Well, there's a lot of fish, actually," he laughed, "but they're just food for the dolphins. You can feed the dolphins yourself, and touch 'em."

Takeru suddenly felt breathless. Though the air-conditioning was on, he was very hot. His heart was pounding.

"What's the matter, Takeru?" asked Mitsuko, sitting next to him in the back seat of the car. She looked into his face anxiously. "Carsick?"

Takeru shook his head. "I'm okay," he said. His voice was weak. "You can't swim with the dolphins, can you?" he asked.

"Don't think so," said Hii-chan.

Takeru seemed relieved. Something that had been blocking his chest began to shrink.

He forced the air from his lungs, trying to get rid of the blockage altogether. But then Hii-chan changed his mind.

"No. Maybe you can…. Yes. You can if ya make a reservation."

"Swim with dolphins?" said Takeru. "You can swim with the dolphins?"

The rearview mirror showed Hii-chan's worried frown.

"What's wrong, Takeru?" he said. "Why're you cryin'?"

Mitsuko put her arm gently around Takeru's quivering shoulders.

"A lot of things've happened…and he's been travelin' since first thing this mornin'. You're tired, Takeru, ain't you?"

Takeru clung to Mitsuko. He tried to curl his body up tight to stop himself from sobbing, but it was no use. There was no controlling it.

"You done well, Takeru," Mitsuko whispered soothingly. "Very well."

At her words a little more of the thing inside him melted away. His tears flowed on.

Remembering the journey from the airport now as he sat in Ken's car, Takeru wanted to cry again.

"When'll you take me?" said Saki again.

"Has your dad said it's 'kay?" asked Ken, raising an eyebrow in the rearview mirror.

"Old Tatsuya wouldn't say no, long as I'm with you," said Saki, echoing Ken's own words from earlier.

"One–nothin'," said Ken with a smile.

Saki peered at the side of Takeru's face.

"You'll come too, won't you?" she said.

"I'll take ya both," said Ken. "How 'bout next Sunday? I'm free."

"Are you sure?" asked Takeru.

"Course," said Ken, nodding. "What's up, Takeru?" he said, suddenly worried. "You don't look happy."

"Keep your eyes on the road, Ken!" shouted Saki. "It ain't safe!"

"What's wrong, Takeru?" said Ken. "You don't wanna go? You scared of dolphins?"

"No I'm not…," said Takeru.

"Really? You 'kay? Feelin' carsick?"

"I'm fine," Takeru said.

But Ken turned on his signal and stopped on the side of the road. A small white truck honked as it came past and Ken sounded his horn in reply. It must have been someone he knew.

Once Ken was sure that Takeru was all right, he started the car again and drove on.

They drove through a series of sharp bends, and then Ken took one hand off the steering wheel and pointed out of the open window.

"There's Lion Cross Point," he said.

He was gesturing toward the tip of a long promontory jutting out into the sea. It was where the coast road took its sharpest turn.

Ken's expression softened for a moment, as if he was remembering something. His large eyes narrowed and a happy smile played on his lips.

"Your ma ever mention Lion Cross Point?"

"No," said Takeru, shaking his head.

Ken looked as though he wanted to say something else, but left it at that.

"You mean 'lion' like 'lions and tigers'?" asked Takeru.

"That's right."

Perhaps the scenery had pushed all the worries out of Takeru's mind. He'd felt cautious about Ken, an unknown man who said he'd known his mother when they were children, but maybe that caution had melted away now—just like the coin had melted away in his hand.

"Does that mean a lion used to cross the sea here?"

"Well…" said Ken, cocking his head. "I doubt it."

"So why is it called Lion Cross Point?"

"I wonder," said Ken. "You're a clever boy. What grade ya say you're in? Fourth? Fifth? You speak very politely. You could learn somethin' from him, Saki."

"Yes sir!" said Saki playfully from the back seat. She straightened her thin back and began to titter, shaking like a flower in the wind.

"Do you do any sports?" asked Ken. "Football or somethin'? That's a Barcelona cap, ain't it?"

"I don't play football," said Takeru.

"Baseball? Or maybe—since you're so polite—judo or kendo?"

"I don't do any sports."

"So Wakako keeps ya studyin' hard then. Strict, is she?"

Takeru said nothing. He felt pain deep inside whenever someone mentioned his mother.

Ken didn't ask any more questions. Maybe he took Takeru's silence as a yes. He glanced at Saki in the rearview mirror.

"Tatsuya ain't so strict is he? He ever been angry with ya? I doubt it!"

"He's always complainin' *you're* too soft," Saki retorted. "Says you spoil me."

"That's the truth," said Ken, laughing.

It was a big hearty laugh, as though to prevent some ill-omened wind from getting into the car. With the windows open, the laugh itself seemed to smell of fish and salt water. It sank away like a wave as they came around the next bend in the road.

"That's the truth," Ken said again. "But still, what do lions gotta do with this place?"

"Maybe there *were* lions here once upon a time," said Saki, baffled.

The question lingered, unresolved, as the car navigated

the bend of Lion Cross Point. The road then straightened as they approached the village of Ogoura on the next bay.

"Wow!" said Takeru.

On some flat ground to the right was a big old boat, its bow facing south. It was just across the road from a two-story concrete building.

"Does that boat ever move?" asked Takeru.

It didn't look as though the boat had been brought there to be repaired. It seemed to be fixed in place with logs and concrete blocks. There were windows in the hull, and curtains visible inside.

"Oh, that!" said Ken. "No, that don't move. It's a guest-house. The Yamato."

It was an old mackerel fishing vessel that had been converted into a guesthouse for people on fishing trips. The Yamato Guesthouse was well known locally.

"Yamato," said Takeru quietly. "Like the Yamato Battleship from the Pacific War?"

"You know a lot," said Ken as they drove past. "The owner's named Yamato Kawakami. He's two years young-er'n me, so he was the same grade as your ma."

Takeru froze, but Ken didn't notice. He kept on talking.

"It was his grandpa's idea t'name him Yamato, they say. His grandpa was in the navy and wanted him named after the battleship."

Takeru was no longer listening. He didn't mean to say anything, but his lips moved, "Ken…"

"Yeah?"

"Were you good friends with my mother?"

"Me and your ma?"

Takeru nodded.

"Course! At your age we played 'gether nearly every day."

Ken's eyes narrowed, as though he were looking at something far away. Did he know that this scenery, steeped in memories, was something Takeru's mother hated? Perhaps he did. His tone suddenly changed.

"Your ma ever mention me?"

Takeru thought for a moment, then, tilting his head, said simply: "I don't remember."

Ken sighed.

"Oh," he said sadly. "Well, no surprise. It was more'n twenty years ago now."

✳

Takeru recalled the stifling heat of the apartment. Upstairs in an old wooden housing block, facing west. The largest window, opposite the entrance, looked out over what people called an orchard, surrounded by indistinguishable houses and other low-rise apartment blocks. He didn't know what sort of trees were in the orchard. Some people said peach. Some said plum. Others said they were grapevines. They had been planted neatly at even spaces, and were about the height of an adult, but

Takeru didn't remember ever seeing fruit on them. In fact, he couldn't remember them having leaves, just bare branches stretching out like the arms of people pretending to be monsters, scaring children. So, to Takeru the orchard wasn't green. It was brown, the color of earth, dry earth. An assembly of blighted trees, standing neatly in line. In a way, they were stranger than monsters.

In the afternoon the sun came directly through the west window. It was hard to bear, especially without curtains, and they didn't have any yet, though they must have been in Akeroma for over six months. His mother was too busy even to go and buy curtains.

The hall led into the kitchen, and beyond that were two tatami-matted rooms. In the farthest room were two unopened cardboard boxes against the wall. At first Takeru thought he might use them as a bed. It seemed like a good idea. But there were no cushions to put on top and use as a mattress, and of course a futon was more comfortable for sleeping anyway.

Takeru soon lost interest in the cardboard boxes, but his brother didn't. His brother was two years older than Takeru, though a similar height. When he wasn't asleep, he often sat quietly on one of the boxes. He sat bent forward, and now and then a thread of saliva fell from his open mouth. Takeru would look away, but sometimes he couldn't fail to see saliva that had hit the floor. An ant crawling around on the tatami would occasionally fall victim to spit falling from the sky. It would writhe around, waving its legs and antennae. With the air so hot, the liquid quickly evaporated, but even so those ants must still have wanted revenge. Takeru wondered if his mother had known that. Though he spent so much time sitting on the hard boxes, his brother never slept on them. Even he knew they wouldn't be comfortable.

There was no air-conditioning in the room and no electric fan. The window was always open, but that just made sleep more difficult. Instead of a breeze it seemed to let in only hot air and the noise of the air-conditioning units on the buildings nearby. At first the two boys had slept on a futon, but it soon grew damp with sweat, so they began to lie directly on the tatami floor.

Takeru continued to use the futon as a pillow, but one day he noticed black marks along its edge. He thought they were ants. Not wanting to be bitten, he tried to squash one with his finger. But no, it wasn't an ant. It was some kind of mark. He stood up and turned the futon over. Both the futon and tatami mat beneath were covered in mold, growths of various sizes. He shivered. He dropped the futon and it fell to the floor with a soft thud. Wisps of cotton stuffing floated up into the air. He decided he'd never use the futon again. He wanted to do something about the mold, but he didn't know what. He looked at his brother, who was sleeping on his stomach as always, his cheek flat against the unswept tatami.

There were black spots on his brother's bare calf. Takeru shuddered. Was his brother developing mold too? He lifted his brother by the shoulders and turned him over. His body was light, far easier to maneuver than Takeru had expected. He looked at the dull-colored skin of his brother's chest and protruding belly. To his relief there was no mold to be seen. The black spots on his brother's calf must have been ants. Takeru was angry. He wanted to squash the ants, but they'd disappeared.

The apartment was on the corner of the block, adjacent to an old concrete building that was being used by a construction company for offices and worker housing. Immediately opposite the window on the north side of the apartment was a grimy sliding window in the other building. It looked almost close enough for an adult to stretch out and touch. Its metal frame was damaged and had been taped. The screen was torn in one corner. At ground level, the gap between the buildings was strewn with empty cans and plastic bags. There were some rain-soaked newspapers and magazines too. The plastic bags quivered, so there must have been wind down there. But no breeze came through the window of the apartment. It had been left open morning, noon, and night and wouldn't close. There must have been too much dust around the frame. An adult might have been able to close it, but it was too hard for a child like Takeru, and it would have been even more difficult for his brother. What if the two of them had tried together? But his brother never came over to give a hand when Takeru was battling with the window. He just lay there with his eyes closed, his bare belly rising and falling. It was hard to tell whether he was sleeping or awake.

How did they live, these two, after their mother had gone? They managed because there was always somebody there to reach out to them. Literally reach out.

One day, that window in the building next door opened and a black arm came out. The hand dropped a cigarette butt. The back of the hand was dark, but the palm was pale. A black face appeared at the window. Takeru couldn't hide his surprise, and the man grinned, widely set teeth standing out white against his dark skin. *Gap-toothed*, thought Takeru.

Takeru had seen him before. He'd been wearing gray-green overalls the first time—it must not have been so hot then. Takeru had been on the way to a convenience store, waiting to cross the road where it ran under the highway.

The sidewalk on the far side of the road was being widened. A dusty, rusting truck was parked there, and the man was walking past it, pushing a wheelbarrow piled with pieces of asphalt ripped up from the road. He looked different than the other workmen. For one thing he was the only one wearing a helmet. It looked very big for his head. What struck Takeru more than that, though, was that his head seemed small for his body—he had a small head but very long limbs. Most remarkable of all was the way he walked, the way his body moved—to Takeru's eyes it seemed to follow a different rhythm than the other men, a different kind of music. He immediately thought he must be foreign. The signal to cross turned green, and just as Takeru reached the other side of the road the man passed close by, now walking in the opposite direction, his wheelbarrow empty. Takeru noticed a smell as the man passed, as though the air were tinged with some kind of spice. He'd seen him again more recently, working on the demolition of a big old house on a busy road not far from the apartment. *There's the African*, Takeru had thought. But he wasn't African. Well, no. He was African but, then again, he wasn't.

Takeru didn't know that the man lived in the building next door. But when he thought about it, the blue truck with filthy mud flaps—the one that was always parked in front of the construction company office—was the same vehicle he'd seen that day on the side of the road. And he knew there were living quarters above the offices. A man who lived there had bought him a can of soda shortly after they'd moved in.

Yes. That's right. That man, the one who bought him a soda, had reached out a helping hand as well. He was from the north—Tohoku—but he said he'd been working in Tokyo for a long time. Takeru forgot his name but it would come back to him later, when he saw Hii-chan standing in front of the vending machine at the gas station in the village by the sea. Not that the man's face had resembled Hii-chan's in the slightest.

Sasaki had had thinning black hair, always combed

48

back over his scalp, and a neat little moustache under his nose. He carried around the sweet smell of hair oil or eau de cologne, mingled with the clean smell of soap. He often bought Takeru a soda at the vending machine by the office entrance. He was soft-spoken and polite.

He said he had a grandson about Takeru's age and that he often bought him soda too. He had to be secretive about it, though, he said, as his daughter would get mad if she found out.

"You're a grandad?" asked Takeru, surprised. It seemed strange. Sasaki certainly wasn't young, but he didn't look old enough to have a grandchild.

"Certainly am," he said. "Will your mom get annoyed if she sees me buying you soda?"

"I think it'll be okay," said Takeru.

Because there's probably no chance of her seeing—is that what Takeru meant?

"Come to think of it, I haven't seen your mom recently. Is she busy?"

Takeru nodded.

"She's a beautiful lady," said Sasaki.

Takeru wondered if Sasaki had ever really seen her. Perhaps he was thinking of someone else.

"She's kind!" Takeru said.

What made him say that? He sounded angry, though Sasaki didn't seem to notice. Or maybe he just pretended not to notice.

"Very, very kind," said Takeru, as though telling himself.

"Is she now?" said Sasaki. "I wonder how old she is. I'd guess about the same age as my daughter…"

Takeru thought for a moment.

"I think she's about thirty," he said vaguely.

"She must have gotten married very young. My daughter married when she was nineteen. She'd just had a baby."

"Can people have babies before they're married?" asked Takeru.

"Babies are born whether their parents are married or not," Sasaki replied, laughing.

Takeru laughed too, to be polite, not knowing what was funny.

Sasaki carried on, in a sadder voice.

"Once she was married she had another baby very quickly, and then right after that she got divorced."

Takeru wanted to know more about Sasaki's grand-children.

"Do the children live with their mother?" he asked.

"They all live in my house," he said.

Sasaki took a cell phone from his pocket and showed Takeru the photo on the screen—his daughter and two grandchildren. His daughter was plump, with dyed-brown hair and narrow eyes. She didn't look much like Sasaki. The boys were chubby too. Their heads were shaved, and they wore matching Pokemon T-shirts (Takeru immedi-ately recognized the monster as Raikou). They looked a lot like their mother.

Sasaki put the cell phone back in his pocket and glanced at the vending machine.

"Does your kid brother want soda too?"

"He's not my kid brother…"

No matter how many times Takeru told him otherwise, Sasaki kept thinking Takeru was the elder brother. It's true that Takeru was slightly taller, and when the two brothers walked together it was Takeru who kept looking back anxiously. It was Takeru who took out the soda cans when they thumped down into the dispensing bin of a vending machine, and it was his brother who waited to be given one. It wasn't just soda that Sasaki bought them. He often got sweets or ice cream for them at the convenience store or supermarket. It was Takeru, of course, who took charge of the plastic bag, and who took something out of it to give to his brother. It was Takeru who, placing the treat in his brother's hand, made him hold it against his chest to keep it from falling. But his brother was the older one and Takeru the younger one.

After a while Sasaki didn't seem to be around anymore. Takeru had often heard him say he was old and wanted to stop working. He must have gone back up north to Tohoku—Aomori, maybe, or Iwate—and be living happily with his daughter and grandsons.

With Sasaki went Sasaki's hands—the hands that passed drinks and snacks to Takeru—small strong hands with thick fingers formed by years of hard manual labor.

And just about the time those hands disappeared, that black arm stretched out from the building next door, that big long-fingered hand.

The strong-featured dark face at the window smiled.

"*Konnichi-wa*," its owner said, Hello.

He continued speaking for a bit, but the only word Takeru understood was Konnichi-wa.

A furrow eventually appeared between the man's eyebrows. He pointed to himself and very slowly said: "Joel."

Takeru, probably staring in amazement, pointed to himself and said: "Takeru."

Joel disappeared for a few moments. Then, coming back, he leaned out of the window and stretched his hand toward Takeru. It was like a big black flower. The long fingers reached close to Takeru's face. They held a plastic bag, and inside the bag were rolls of bread.

At first Takeru didn't understand.

"*Tabete*," said Joel, Eat. He swung the bag gently. It rustled.

Takeru clasped the bag with both hands.

"*Arigato*," he said quietly.

Joel's long-lashed eyes gleamed happily.

To make sure he was understood, Takeru, very shyly, almost inaudibly, spoke again:

"Thank you," he said in English.

Joel's smile broadened.

"*Chotto matte!*" he said, Wait a second. He disappeared again.

"*Nonde*," he said, coming back, Drink. He held out a two-liter bottle of Fanta Orange.

His long fingers reached almost all the way around the bottle.

"Thank you!" said Takeru, hugging it to his chest. He might have been holding a baby.

Joel appeared at the window often after that, and passed Takeru bread, rice balls, and drinks. Takeru didn't really know how to react, so he always accepted them in silence. Well, not exactly silence: he never forgot to say *thank you* or *arigato*. He and his brother savored every mouthful. No. They gobbled it all down like animals.

Takeru had no idea why the African man next door would be so kind to them. Perhaps all African people were like that. There'd been a boy named Daisuke Jones in sixth grade at Takeru's school in Momono. He had coffee-colored skin and curly hair, and everyone called him DJ. Takeru and DJ were in a group of kids who walked to school together. DJ was always very kind to the younger children. He sometimes gave Takeru and the others rides on his shoulders. He was 180 centimeters tall and it felt amazingly high up there. When the children called him the Tokyo Sky Tree, which was then being built, he said no, he was the Sears Tower. He told them proudly that his daddy came from the city where President Obama used to work.

But Joel wasn't African. He had said so himself. No, Takeru didn't understand what Joel said. But one day Joel had shown him a map through the window. He unfolded it from a travel guide he'd gotten a hold of somewhere. The map showed a lot of islands in the ocean. In the area that Joel pointed to were names like "Haiti" and "Jamaica," and, in bigger letters, "Gulf of Mexico" and "Caribbean Sea." The coast of Africa was far away on the right-hand side of the map, all the way across the Atlantic.

The name *Haiti* reminded Takeru of Heidi, the little girl from the Swiss Alps. He also thought of Haiji, a classmate of his in first and second grades at Momono Elementary. Their names may have been similar, but Haiji was a big boy with a sharp, tanned face. He looked nothing like apple-cheeked Heidi, with her bright-colored clothes. They both had high-pitched voices, though, and laughed a lot. They both ran fast.

Takeru had heard of Jamaica of course. That was where Usain Bolt came from. In a way slim long-limbed Joel looked a little like Bolt to Takeru.

The semester after the Beijing Olympics, the boys at school were always striking the bow-pulling pose before running during breaks or in P.E. class.

Takeru did it too, of course, not that it made him run any faster. Some of the older boys did it before their races on Field Day that autumn, and the spectators all cheered. Takeru hadn't been chosen for the relay and always came last or second-to-last in his individual race. *I hope my mother doesn't see*, he thought. But there was no chance of that. She had never come to a field day. Not once.

There were no school lunches on Field Day. Takeru's mother didn't give him a packed lunch, though. Instead, he was given some money to buy something at a convenience store. He didn't tell anybody he didn't have his own packed lunch. So how did anyone know?

When he arrived at the classroom that morning, Haruka Yuasa came over to him. She was a quiet girl, with short hair and round glasses. People said her grandparents owned the fields around the school. According to girls in the class who'd been over there to play, her family had a very big house. The grounds were vast, they said, with a storehouse and barn, and an officially protected keyaki elm that was over two hundred years old. The house also had a very rare old-fashioned veranda. Takeru had no clear image of what a veranda was then. He would suddenly remember Haruka one evening when he was having supper on the veranda at Mitsuko's house. He'd feel a lump in his chest and want to cry—not knowing whether it was from happiness or sadness. Although he was in the same class as Haruka, they'd never been paired up or even put in the same group. He couldn't remember speaking to her more than once or twice before.

"Takeru," she said, coming up to his desk, "this is for you."

She spoke in a hushed voice, as though confessing something she didn't want anyone else to hear. Takeru looked down. On the desk she'd put something wrapped in a *furoshiki* cloth, tied firmly at the top. It was the shape of a small box.

"Lunch," she said.

Being Field Day, the hubbub in the classroom was louder than normal, so her voice was almost completely drowned out. Her face was bright red, her breaths short and trembling. Takeru began to worry that the heat from her face and breath would steam up her glasses.

His own face was probably just as red as hers, his breathing just as awkward. He kept his eyes down. His ears pounded, his brain burning like an overheated motor. But he heard what she said:

"Take it. It's from my mother. She told me to give it to you."

For a moment Takeru couldn't think at all. No, not just for a moment. It lasted much longer than that. Looking back, he couldn't recall much from that day. He couldn't remember what place he came in the race (probably last), or whether he'd managed the dance steps correctly (he wouldn't have), or even what team he was on—red or white.

One thing he did remember though was that someone else had also been given a lunch box. Takeru saw Haruka take a similar bundle to Takuto Watanabe, a boy whose mother was from the Philippines. She didn't seem to get quite as red when she gave the bundle to Takuto. People said Haruka went to church every Sunday, and Takuto wore a crucifix pendant—maybe that had something to do with it.

There was a little *jizo* shrine on the main street, where the cherry trees were beautiful in spring. In most places jizo—stone Buddhist figures that look like child monks—are given plain red bonnets and aprons. But at this shrine, somebody dressed them in pinks and yellows, with Hello Kitty or Miffy patterns. (Takeru would have preferred to see the jizo dressed in Pokemon patterns—Pikachu or Piplup.) Takeru heard that the shrine was on land owned by Haruka's family. *They own everything around here*, he thought. Perhaps they owned the church too. It seemed strange to Takeru that a church and a jizo shrine might be associated in that way. To him they seemed like things that had no connection whatsoever. It was much later, in the graveyard by the sea, that he imagined a jizo with a crucifix around its neck. The idea made him smile. There were no bonnets or aprons on the jizo in that graveyard—just dull green lichen and scabies-like patterns on their bodies and heads formed by wind and rain. Their faces were flat and featureless.

Another thing he clearly remembered about the field day was that he'd hardly been able to eat any of the food he'd been given. Had he been full? No chance of that. He was always hungry. Children whose families were with them had lunch in the school yard or gym. Those with no visitors—like Takeru and Takuto Watanabe—ate in the classrooms. Takeru opened the bundle that Haruka had given him, thinking he should leave some to take home for his brother. He must have had an inkling, though, of what he'd find. His bundle was bigger than Takuto's. It was twice as thick. He must have noticed that. And when he opened it he discovered not just an ordinary lunch box, but one that had two layers. Both layers contained the same food—most of the space on each layer was taken up by two large sushi rolls, the remaining third by a combination of fried egg, fried chicken, sausage, asparagus wrapped in bacon, and broccoli. It looked fantastic. An amazing lunch! But Takeru had no appetite. Some strange, heavy lump was blocking his throat, his stomach. He stretched quietly across to take a look at Takuto's box, but it was too far away to see. Maybe his sight was blurred by tears. Still, there must have been the same food in Takuto's box. But Takeru had been given two portions, specially wrapped up in a single cloth. *Give this to Takeru*, Haruka's mother had told her. That was obvious. Like Takuto, Takeru was one of the smallest and thinnest children in the class. Did he look like someone who would eat so much? Maybe he did! Someone who ate endlessly, but stayed thin. No. Takeru was just kidding himself. Nobody would think that. The truth was staring him in the face. But how had Haruka's mother known about his brother? Chopsticks motionless in his hand, Takeru stared down at the layered box, but he didn't really see it. Somebody was thinking about his brother. Did this make him happy? Was that why he was crying? Or was it despair? Despair that something that shouldn't be known, something that mustn't be known, something that his mother probably, no, definitely, was trying to hide, had not been successfully concealed?

Still holding the chopsticks, Takeru wiped his eyes with the back of his hand and looked up. Takuto was staring at him anxiously. The moment Takeru caught his gaze, Takuto hurriedly turned his large eyes away and carried on eating, as though nothing had happened.

It can't have been easy for Haruka to come to school carrying bundles for Takuto and Takeru (and his brother) in addition to her own things. Takeru tried to imagine how he'd have felt if it had been him doing that. He'd have been on edge, worried that other children might ask what the bundles were for. Haruka Yuasa wasn't like that, though. She didn't cower. She may have been red in the face and her breathing may have been awkward, but embarrassment didn't defeat her. There was always something wrapped around her, something big that accepted her and supported her when she faltered.

It wasn't her family's big house. It wasn't all the land they owned. It was something much bigger than either of those, so big it didn't even stand comparison. It must be Haruka's mother, Takeru thought. And it must be something in the church they went to together on Sundays. If Takeru had been told to take lunch for one of his classmates he'd have refused, thinking it was stupid, that *he'd* look stupid. But luckily (was it really lucky?) he didn't have the kind of mother who'd prepare lunch for his classmates and make him bring it. In fact, he didn't even have a mother who made lunch for her own child. Not having that kind of mother, Takeru didn't recognize that big thing at all. He had no way of knowing. It's reasonable to say that, isn't it? Because to Takeru this big thing was maternal, something that was bound up with motherhood.

But Takeru was wrong. The big thing didn't have to be in a mother (though of course it could be), and it wasn't always necessarily linked to a church. You could say it was connected in a way to the jizo shrines, but also unconnected. Takeru would realize all this after he went to live with Mitsuko in the village by the sea. Mitsuko's beliefs in God or Buddha were no stronger than anyone else's, but this thing was always with her.

In fact, the little village was full of it. So why had Takeru's mother said she hated the place? Why had she wanted to get away as soon as she could?

And the big thing wasn't only in this narrow stretch of land by the sea. No. It was everywhere. If it wasn't, why had Sasaki and Joel helped Takeru and his brother? Why, simply living next door, did they reach out their hands—those hands so different in shape, color, and size, yet, in the care they showed to defenseless things, identical? Maybe this thing was not just in the atmosphere, wrapping itself around people—perhaps it could come and go freely in people's hearts. It was surely this that had made Haruka's mother notice Takeru and his brother. It was this that had brought to Joel's attention the apartment in the next-door building, the clear signs of habitation there, even though the lights were never on, even at night. It wasn't by chance that Joel and the boy saw each other that day. After getting off work early Joel had spent time watching the open window next door, as though waiting for little animals to come out of their burrow. He had bread, drinks, and fruit—not much, but some. Maybe for him it was like feeding animals. Or maybe it wasn't.

Did Takeru realize that Joel watched over them?

One late afternoon, Takeru was sitting on a broken bench in the overgrown backyard of the apartment block. He was reading a magazine he'd found lying around somewhere. He looked up. The sky above the orchard to the west was tinted orange. He noticed a shiny black car pull up on the road by the orchard fence. Normally he didn't pay attention to what cars were parked nearby, but this time he did. He felt a kind of premonition. Maybe the big thing was telling him something. The moment the man got out of the car, Takeru's blood froze. He felt cold sweat streaming down his back.

It was him.

Takeru's mother called him Kazuhiro—and sometimes "Kazuhiro*h*," extending the final syllable in a wheedling, girlish voice. Takeru would think of this nightmare of a man when, in the village by the sea, he first heard the cry of a deer, *kani-hiro-*. It was like his mother's voice when she called *Kazuhiroh*. According to Mitsuko, though, the cry was that of a buck calling to a doe, not the other way around.

Kazuhiro didn't look frightening in the least. In fact he almost looked kind. He was slim and muscular, with narrow hips. He had short spikey hair, and his eyebrows were neatly plucked and trimmed, his eyes deep-set. Sometimes there were Band-Aids around his eyes. Takeru remembered him—or was it his mother?—telling him that he boxed or something. He had a gold necklace, a large black shiny watch, and bracelets. He wore chunky rings on his fingers.

He was always very neatly dressed. If he came inside their apartment in Momono he'd immediately start to look uncomfortable, checking the bottoms of his socks.

If he saw any dirt or dust he'd click his tongue. "It's filthy in here," he'd say. "And it stinks of garbage. Do some cleaning!" "Sorry Kazuhir*oh*!" Takeru's mother would say. Or "I know, I'll do it properly next time!" But she'd never done it properly before. And she wouldn't now.

One day, Kazuhiro's patience snapped. His eyes flashed with rage. He leaned down and picked up a wooden hanger from a pile of laundry that had been lying unfolded on the floor for days.

"How can I get it into your head? I told you to clean

up, so clean the fuck up! How many times do I have to say it, you stupid whore?"

He spat out the words in a fury and then, as Takeru's mother wearily pushed the laundry together with her foot, he brought the wooden hanger down on her head with a crack. The boys were right there. Takeru saw it. Did his brother? Did he understand what he saw?

Takeru's head swam. He didn't know if his brother was tense. He can't recall what expression was on his mother's face, but then he doesn't remember her face at all. He does remember her sinking silently to the floor though, her hands clasped to her head, crimson oozing from the gaps between her fingers. Did Takeru hurl himself at Kazuhiro to protect his mother? He couldn't move. His knees were shaking. He was petrified. He imagined the hanger being brought down on his own head. He felt he was about to pee. Maybe he did pee. With Takeru in such a state, wouldn't it have been reasonable for his brother to cry out? Wouldn't it have been reasonable, with spittle still dribbling from his mouth, for him miraculously to face up to the man who'd injured his mother? But of course that is a miracle that didn't happen.

The violence continued. Takeru's mother was hit by a glass and an ashtray thrown across the room. She was punched by a thick-ringed fist. She was kicked in the belly and back as she cowered on the floor, unable to speak out of fear and pain. Even then no miracle happened. Maybe Takeru wanted to punish her. Why? Because whenever this storm of a young man came or left, it was as though their sudden fights had never happened. She would nestle up to him. "Kazuhiroh," she'd say in that wheedling voice—a doe calling to a buck. She spent hours happily making herself up for him, putting on her favorite clothes. There was no space to walk on the floor; it was always strewn with crumpled tissues and tester packets of makeup, so many that he wondered where they came from. There were bottles of mascara and nail polish; tubes and jars and powdery brushes both big and small; clothes she'd ultimately decided not to wear, coils of discarded tights. Sometimes she wore big showy sunglasses, like locust eyes, to hide her bruises. She'd leave a thousand-yen note by the door, telling Takeru to get some prepackaged meals at the convenience store, and then she'd run downstairs to meet the man waiting outside in his fancy foreign car. The low hum of its engine welled up from the depths of the earth, making the air tremble. The thousand-yen note stank of her perfume, though it had only been in his mother's hand for a moment. The smell spread to Takeru's fingers and he put them under his brother's nose. Did his nostrils flinch? Was there a change in his eyes? Any flicker of happiness or disgust?

He would think of his brother's eyes the day Hii-chan took him out to fish on the floating quay that stretched a hundred meters out into the bay.

"There're some sea turtles in there," said Hii-chan, pointing down into the fish pen. "Someone caught 'em."

Takeru looked excitedly into the fish pen, but the water was dark and he couldn't see to the bottom. He couldn't sense any movement, but as though trying to convince himself that he could, he pointed to the corner of the pen.

"Looks like there's something over there," he said to Hii-chan.

The water wasn't showing him what he wanted to see. *It's my brother's eyes*, he thought. It reflected the sky and hills, and along with them the quay, the boats, and Takeru himself. Yes, his brother was staring up at him, seeing him as part of this land—the land his mother hated, detested.

"You must be sick of living in this pigsty," Kazuhiro said to Takeru once, when he'd grown tired of shouting at Takeru's mother.

Pigs are very clean was what Takeru wanted to say. Had he been too frightened? He didn't know whether that was true or not about pigs—it was something he'd heard someone say on TV.

Later, living with Mitsuko in the village by the sea, he'd remember that day and be glad he hadn't said it.

Hii-chan wanted to take every opportunity to show Takeru things he wouldn't have been able to see in Tokyo.

He took him all over the place. Takeru would hear a small truck pull up behind Mitsuko's house, then the sound of footsteps on the gravel, and he'd know it was Hii-chan. One day Hii-chan took him to visit a friend who kept pigs on the edge of the village. The pigsty was in a grove of cedar trees sloping upward behind the friend's two-story concrete house. The pigs' fat bodies were covered in mud, feces, and urine. As Takeru covered his nose and mouth to keep out the stench, he felt very relieved he hadn't told Kazuhiro that pigs were clean.

"Your fucking mother amazes me! She just doesn't get it. You're at school now, so you're old enough to help her. You have to do it—she's too fucking dumb."

Kazuhiro glanced across the room at Takeru's brother. He shook his head, his mouth twisted in a smile of bafflement and contempt.

"No point telling him. He wouldn't understand a fucking word!"

"I'll kill you!"

Takeru felt like he'd shouted it, but the words just reverberated inside his head. He hated hearing his mother insulted. Of course he did. But maybe what he really couldn't stand was having his brother spoken of like that.

"I'll kill you!"

The shout inside him was so loud he thought his eardrums might burst. He wanted to shout like Kazuhiro and his mother did when they were arguing, hurling abuse back and forth so loud he wondered if their throats might rip apart. But all that shouting meant nothing. That was clear. Because after Kazuhiro and his mother abused each other with the foulest possible language—the types of words that his teacher said made dictionaries weep—they always ended up lying happily side by side.

One day, when Takeru got home from school, he heard his mother gasping and shouting in pain, a man swearing frenziedly. Takeru's heart beat against his ribs. As he came down the hallway he could hear violent breathing from the tatami room where the family slept (no…his mother hardly ever slept with Takeru and his brother). There was a narrow gap between the sliding door and the frame. Takeru caught a glimpse…thought he caught a glimpse of them, biting and tearing like animals, bodies entwined, "Kill me!" his mother screamed. Her voice seemed cornered by despair. "Kill me!"

Takeru was terrified. He ran out of the apartment and down the rusting staircase. His mouth was dry. He retraced his route toward school, still carrying his backpack.

Then he remembered.

What about his brother?

He'd left his brother in the apartment. The blue sky lurched toward him. The ground shook at his feet. The sky and earth were attacking him. What terrible scene had his brother witnessed? Had he been caught up in the killing?

But Takeru couldn't go back right away. He walked as

far as Zebra Park, a playground next to the public housing he passed on the way to school. Children called it Zebra Park because of a plastic zebra for toddlers next to the swings. There was a plastic horse and a plastic giraffe as well. Some children called it Giraffe Park, but nobody called it Horse Park. Some boys, mostly older than him, were playing football. He leaned against an iron post and watched them for a while. He thought he should go home, but decided to wait until one side scored again. But neither did. Three of the boys started arguing about which one of them was Lionel Messi. Two were wearing Messi's Barcelona jersey, but the third was dressed as a Japanese national player. It would be nice if Messi played for Japan, thought Takeru vaguely. The PA system broadcast the five o'clock chimes. The game broke up without the goal he'd been waiting for—perhaps it was time to stop, or maybe the boys were just getting bored. The blue sky above the public housing was deepening toward purple. Takeru left the park and came out onto the sidewalk. There was a flicker above his head and the streetlight came on. He could smell cooking coming from the houses as he walked sluggishly down the street. Was his brother all right? For some reason he thought of his brother first, not his mother. He was angry with himself for having abandoned him.

He sighed as he reached for the doorknob—a sigh so harsh and heavy that it hurt. He nervously turned the knob, but the door was locked. He took the key that hung on a string around his neck and put it into the keyhole.

The apartment was silent. He stepped toward the room from which he'd heard the terrifying voices of his mother and the man entwined together (he probably knew what was really happening). He peered in. His brother was lying on his stomach, half on and half off a futon, sheets and covers in chaos. But there was no blood. Takeru's own breathing was so loud he couldn't tell if his brother was breathing or not, but he could see some movement in his brother's back. His cheek was squashed against the tatami, his lips puckered. Takeru put his hand against his brother's mouth and felt warm, damp breath.

He sighed with relief. His brother was okay.

Even if he did know what had been going on between his mother and the man, he was probably still worried about his brother. There was no more pretense in that feeling than in his regret at having left him there alone. An ant was crawling on his brother's arm, so Takeru squashed it with a crumpled tissue from the floor. He looked at the tissue. The ant's tiny body seemed to have produced a large mass of sticky, ugly-smelling fluid.

Takeru was exhausted. He lay down beside his brother and pressed close. His brother's body was warm. Takeru slept.

When he woke it was dark. He turned on the light. His brother was still asleep. After a while, he heard the sound of a car stopping on the road outside. The engine didn't sound at all like Kazuhiro's car. Takeru went out onto the balcony and leaned over to look down at the road. He was right. Kazuhiro's was a stylish black foreign car—this one was white and Japanese. Takeru knew Kazuhiro took very good care of his car—it was always sparkling clean. Takeru had never been inside it, and, of course, his brother hadn't either. He'd once seen it parked on a side road some distance away from the apartment. He'd had a ten-yen coin in his pocket and thought about using it to scratch the dark gleaming chassis. But then he remembered his mother saying the car had cost eight million yen. He hesitated. If it cost that much, it might make more sense to use a big five-hundred-yen coin. Then he began to worry about what would happen if Kazuhiro found out. The thought made him tremble, so he gave up on the idea and walked away. But he made a wish. He wished with all his might that Kazuhiro's smart black car would be smashed in an accident. Seeing the white car outside the apartment didn't make him think that his wish had come true, though. The car belonged to someone else—he knew that. Sure, his mother got out. But the man who climbed out of the driver's side wasn't Kazuhiro. The man took some paper bags from the back seat and followed Takeru's mother up the stairs.

His mother called him Nakayama-san. He was a square-faced, balding man. He was stocky and paunchy, and wore black-framed glasses. Takeru's mother said he worked for the council's welfare department. Takeru couldn't imagine where his mother would have met someone from the council. Nakayama often drove his mother home to the apartment in that white car. They held hands and linked arms. Nakayama sometimes brought sushi or cakes. There was probably something like that in one of the paper bags he'd just taken out of the car.

When Nakayama came into the apartment Takeru's mother would offer to make tea, but he would stop her. Instead, he'd go into the little kitchen, boil some water himself, and make instant coffee. Takeru was always nervous that Nakayama might get angry about the state of the apartment, and one day Nakayama seemed to notice Takeru's worried look.

"This is nothing," he said calmly. "My place is much worse. It's a pigsty."

"I thought pigs were clean," Takeru said. It seemed okay to say it to Nakayama.

"Oh, yeah. I'm sorry," Nakayama said. "I wasn't being fair to pigs. But my kids leave their manga and toys all over the place. They never clear them up, no matter what I say."

Nakayama sighed.

"What grades are your children in, sir?" Takeru asked, when his mother had gone to the bathroom.

"The girl's in her second year of junior high, and the boy's in fifth grade," Nakayama said, looking rather embarrassed.

"Is he at Momono?"

"No, it would be nice if he was, though. He's at Yamashiro First."

Nakayama had a gentle, low-pitched voice—very different from Kazuhiro's shrillness. But when they panted and groaned they sounded exactly the same. Everyone must sound the same when they're writhing in pain, Takeru thought, or close to death. Perhaps animals too. Had it been Nakayama with his mother earlier, shouting, writhing, clinging? But what about that "Kill me!"? Would his mother say that to Nakayama?

One day Nakayama and Takeru were alone together in the kitchen. Nakayama was drinking coffee as always, the little table strewn with empty prepackaged meal containers and instant noodle bowls.

"Takeru," he said suddenly, "do you want to go to the aquarium next Sunday?"

"The aquarium?" The excitement in Takeru's eyes soon abated. "Do you mean with your kids, Mr. Nakayama? Would we all go together?"

Nakayama shook his head as he sipped his coffee.

"My daughter's in a brass-band competition that day, and my son's got a football match. My wife's going to go watch him play."

"Don't you have to go too, Sir?"

Nakayama smiled.

"It'll be okay," he said.

Takeru was standing at the entrance to the tatami

room. He glanced over his shoulder.

"Of course," said Nakayama. "I'll take you both."

The narrow eyes behind the thick lenses narrowed further. Nakayama looked troubled by something.

"Takeru," he said.

"Yes, Mr. Nakayama?"

"You don't have to be so polite when you talk to me. It's too formal. It makes me uncomfortable."

If Takeru had spoken to Kazuhiro in an informal way, he would have been in trouble. He'd have gotten a sharp smack on the head, or his cheek would have been pinched and twisted—as painful as a burn. In fact he *had* been burned once with a cigarette. He'd seen his mother punched and kicked and hadn't been able to control himself:

"You stupid man!" he'd said. "Drop dead!"

Because he'd seen his mother punched and kicked? Is that why? Wasn't it how the man looked at his brother, the way he tapped his brother on the head, as if to imply he wasn't worth hitting properly? "You stupid man!" Takeru had muttered. "Drop dead!" Kazuhiro heard him. He threw Takeru to the floor and sat on him. He pinned Takeru's arms with his knees and slapped his cheeks, first left then right. "Talk to me like that would you?" he said, spitting the words down at Takeru's face. He took his lit cigarette and pressed it into the flesh at either side of Takeru's mouth.

Takeru's body convulsed. He'd remember this later

when Ken Shiomi took him to see the yellowtail farmers at work in the bay. As he watched the fish being held down and gutted he'd remember writhing in desperation under Kazuhiro. The fish pens by the quay frothing and bubbling, torrents of water tumbling down from the nets as they were hauled high in the air by cranes. Takeru stared up at them, hypnotized. But now he was staring up at Kazuhiro. He didn't regret what he'd said. He burned with hatred for this man who was too contemptuous to pin down and punch his brother, but who'd been on top of his mother and was now on him. Takeru's mouth, burned on both sides by the cigarette, shouted just what his mother had shouted: "Kill me!" What was it that was grasped and squeezed flat in the man's hand? Was it the cheek of a defiant child, or was it the naked white breast of a woman, the tip of its dark nipple sticking up between the man's fingers? He didn't know. Was it Takeru's voice shouting, or his mother's? He didn't know. But it certainly, definitely, wasn't his brother's.

"What's the matter, Takeru?"

Nakayama's concerned voice broke Takeru's trance.

Takeru shook his head. He tried to say something, but his throat was dry. His tongue seemed to be stuck to the roof of his mouth. He ran his hand over his lips. The burn marks had almost disappeared now, but for a while he'd been unable to talk. Even smiling had been painful—stretching, breaking the healing wounds. He moved his mouth cautiously, as though the pain might return. But speaking without formality was easier than he'd imagined.

"The aquarium—you mean the place with the dolphin show?"

"Yes," said Nakayama, nodding happily.

"Wow! That'd be great," said Takeru. He wasn't just saying it. He wanted to go.

"Okay. Let's go next week. It's a date."

"Yeah! Great! Thank you."

He'd been wanting to go to the aquarium for a long time. They had sea otters, penguins, and a huge tank where whale sharks swam around. What Takeru really wanted to see, though, were the dolphins. It wasn't just a dolphin show—jumping through hoops and throwing balls with their noses—you could actually swim with them. His classmate Ippei Shimizu had been several times. He said it was amazingly fun and the dolphins were really smart. The other kids called Ippei "Animal Professor." He always spent his breaks looking at books about wildlife, and knew a lot about it. His desk was next to Takeru's for a while and he often showed him whatever book he was reading. Takeru found out something very important from Ippei: There was a bottle-nosed dolphin at the aquarium named Johnnie, and Ippei told Takeru that Johnnie had special healing powers and could get children to open up. By coming into contact with Johnnie, swimming with him in the water, children who'd never spoken before would start to talk.

Takeru didn't believe it at first. For one thing, how could those children swim? It seemed unlikely that children who were so cut off that they couldn't speak would be able to swim. "Oh, I'm so sorry," said Ippei, speaking as if he were an adult. "I didn't explain it well. The kids are held in the water by the staff or their parents while Johnnie swims around them. He never takes his eyes off the child, and once he's circled several times he swims in closer. He brings his long mouth right up to the child's face and makes a noise—it's as though he's talking to the child, or maybe chanting or singing. And then a miracle happens…" Takeru was still a bit skeptical, but Ippei insisted it was true—and Ippei's father was a doctor—so Takeru decided to believe him.

What if Johnnie and his brother could swim together? What if…

He waited eagerly for the day of the visit.

But the day never came, and it was all Takeru's fault.

When Nakayama finished his coffee, he'd always stand up and carefully wash the cup in the sink before he left. He'd say goodbye to Takeru's mother, embracing her by the front door without bothering to check whether Takeru was looking. He always said goodbye to Takeru too, and, most importantly for Takeru, said goodbye to his brother as well. Perhaps that was why Takeru thought Nakayama was a nice person. When he got up in the morning and found Nakayama drinking instant coffee in the kitchen, he was never particularly bothered that he'd stayed the night. Rather, he was worried about what might happen if Kazuhiro found out.

And he did. Because Nakayama forgot to wash a cup. Was that why? If it was—if Kazuhiro had sensed Nakayama's existence from the cup on the table, if that was really how he found out Takeru's mother had another man—then it was all Takeru's fault.

Yes. It was all his fault. When Nakayama left that day Takeru noticed he hadn't picked up the cup as he normally did. In other words Takeru noticed that he didn't wash it. But Takeru didn't tell him. He should have. He'd noticed, so he should have said something. But was it really, truly because of the cup?

There was no point in wondering about that now. He was to blame. It was all his fault that he, and therefore of course his brother, couldn't go to the aquarium.

In the middle of the night Takeru heard the ominous vibration of Kazuhiro's engine in the street. It sounded angrier, more menacing than ever. The car door slammed. Takeru heard his mother fall down on the road. When she came in, her face was almost unrecognizable. There were cigarette burns on her arms. Takeru burst into tears. His mother cried too. Her eyelids were swollen purple-red, her eyes could hardly open, and beneath them ran streaks of tears and blood. His brother didn't cry, though. He just stood motionless behind Takeru. If he'd swum with Johnnie he'd be crying now—the three of them would be able to cry together. He'd be capable of crying. Takeru had made that miracle impossible. He sobbed uncontrollably. His mother put her arms around the two boys and hugged them. Or rather, she clung to them. Takeru had not been held like that for a very long time.

After that, his mother decided to escape Kazuhiro. They moved from Momono to Akeroma in the next prefecture. Really she should have gone farther. The problem was finding somewhere. They chose Akeroma because Nakayama had a friend who ran a real estate agency there. Nakayama had asked him if he had any ideas, and he suggested the apartment block. The landlord had a lot of property in the area. He owned a number of similar buildings, some parking lots, and he had recently bought some newer condominiums as well. He also owned the orchard. Some of his apartment buildings were over thirty years old and had very few tenants. He'd asked Nakayama's real estate agent friend to handle all of them for him. The agent had told them that, given the situation, it didn't matter if the rent wasn't always paid on time. "It's just a kind of hobby for the owner," he said. "I don't think he'd notice."

The landlord may not have been very conscious of his tenants, but Kazuhiro quickly sniffed them out.

It was he that had just climbed out of the foreign car parked by the orchard. Kazuhiro. No question about it.

Takeru ran up the rusty staircase, the manga book hugged to his chest. There were five apartments on each of the two floors of the building, but the only occupied one was theirs, on the second floor at the northern end. He went inside and locked the door. Fortunately, the lights were off. Maybe Kazuhiro wouldn't notice the apartment. He looked in on his brother—sleeping in his underwear in one of the tatami rooms. He'd always slept a lot, but recently he spent almost all day fast asleep. There was no fear of him making a noise. Takeru pressed himself against the wall and, trying to keep his face out of view, peered through the corner of the window. Kazuhiro was coming closer. *We're finished*, Takeru thought.

Then something entirely unexpected happened. As Kazuhiro reached the block's unused, overgrown parking lot, someone suddenly called out to him from behind. He turned around. It was Joel, supermarket bags hanging from his long arms. He was at least a head taller than Kazuhiro. Kazuhiro was clearly astonished to be called to by a black man.

"Where are you going?" asked Joel in Japanese. "No entry!"

"I go tsu my garlfrend," Kazuhiro said in English. This attempt at a foreign language seemed to make his voice even higher than usual. He was gesticulating pointlessly with his hands, his silver rings and gold bracelet glittering in the setting sun. Joel didn't seem to understand what he was saying.

"Boy…meetsu…garlu!" Kazuhiro shouted desperately

in English, then in Japanese, "Why the fuck can't you understand?"

"No one there," said Joel in Japanese. "No entry!"

"What?" said Kazuhiro in his own language. "You speak Japanese?" He was so tense he hadn't noticed before.

"No one there."

"Is that right?" said Kazuhiro, raising his sharp eyebrows suspiciously. He looked up at Joel.

"Soon demolish," said Joel, pointing at the excavator on the construction site. "Danger!"

"You work for the developer?" Kazuhiro said. "We're in the same business, you and me. Comrades! Colleagues! Come on, let me take a look around."

"Danger," said Joel, looking down at Kazuhiro. "Can't go in."

"Come on, my friend. Just a little look. Okay?"

Joel waved his big hand dismissively.

"Nobody there. Danger. Collapse. Can't go in."

Kazuhiro wavered in the face of Joel's stubborn resolve.

"Okay. I've got the wrong place. Understood," he said. And then in English: "Sank you. Sank you bery muchi!"

He went back to his car. Its chassis and wheels shone faintly in the evening light. Joel stayed standing in front of the block until the car drove off. His long shadow reached all the way to where Takeru was hiding in silence upstairs. Joel turned and waved up at the window.

Then he disappeared from view around the corner of the building. A moment later Takeru heard footsteps on the stairs. He opened the door. Joel was standing outside.

"*Konnichi-wa*," said Joel, and handed Takeru a large plastic bag.

"Thank you," said Takeru, taking the bag. It was heavy.

Inside were sweet rolls, apples, aloe-flavored yogurt, and a carton of milk. Once he'd taken the bag, Takeru noticed that Joel was carrying another, smaller one. Joel put his big hand inside and pulled out a red baseball-style cap. On it was the Manchester United emblem. Joel placed the cap gently on Takeru's head. It was slightly too big. Joel put his hand on top of the cap and adjusted its position.

"Thank you!" said Takeru. He tried to look up at Joel, but the cap slid forward over his face and he couldn't see anything. He burst out laughing. Joel gently pushed the brim up again and then pulled another cap out of the bag.

"*Pour ton frère.*"

It was dark blue and had the FC Barcelona emblem.

"What?" asked Takeru.

"For your little brother," said Joel in Japanese.

"Thank you!" Takeru said, worrying that his smile might look forced.

Obviously Joel, like the others, thought Takeru was the older of the two boys. Even so, Takeru was happy.

Joel had saved them. But how had he known

Kazuhiro was looking for their mother? It all seemed odd to Takeru. But maybe for Joel the situation was quite simple. A young boy sat on the rusty old cast-iron bench reading manga, swinging his legs happily. Suddenly he froze. His face turned pale. He was looking at a man with spiky hair, precious metal adorning his neck and hands—a gangster, obviously. In just a glance Joel would have seen that Takeru was frightened, that he was trying to get away. But why would he want to protect Takeru? What made him do it? It had to be the same big thing that had been protecting Takeru all along—protecting him and his brother. The big thing—far, far bigger than the almost two-meter-tall Joel—had told him to keep an eye on the two brothers, to keep watch over them as they lived in the ramshackle old building next door, as good as abandoned by their mother. It had to be that. But if that big thing gave strength to those around him, why in the end did it abandon Takeru?

Kazuhiro had gone, but he could easily turn up again. Takeru was scared. He was worried for Joel too. Kazuhiro had backed down that day, overawed by the larger man, but he was a very jealous person and might start thinking there was something between Joel and Takeru's mother. After that day, Takeru thought he saw Kazuhiro's car several times in the area. Perhaps it was just a similar car, or maybe it was his imagination, but still he didn't think Kazuhiro was somebody who'd give up easily.

Joel continued to pass food to Takeru through the windows, and sometimes brought it to the apartment. The days were shorter now, and the weather was getting cold. Joel had brought over some blankets, but even with them it was cold inside the apartment. Takeru wandered the streets in search of warmth—supermarkets, convenience stores. He didn't like to visit the same places all the time, so sometimes he went a long way away. Public libraries were perfect to spend time in, but he had to be careful not to go during school hours. If people started noticing him, he moved on before they asked any questions.

He often went to a big supermarket a twenty-minute walk down the main road. They had started playing Christmas songs. He couldn't remember exactly when. He was always hungry; his stomach rumbled. He couldn't think clearly about anything—his mind rotated like an empty dryer. He probably went to the supermarket because the old woman was there. It was a large store, and next to an in-store bakery at the back was an area for shoppers to sit and relax. There were three sets of tables and chairs in the middle, and against the bakery wall was a false-leather banquette and four identical Formica tables. By the plate glass on the opposite side were a vending machine, an ice machine, a photocopier, and a blood-pressure gauge that you could use for free. Takeru always sat on the banquette, reading an old manga book. Nobody complained. He'd often see men on their own there, middle-aged or older, unmarried, he guessed, eating lunch from boxes or snacks they'd bought in the store. He'd see mothers with children and heavy bags, chatting happily, telling their chubby children not to climb on the seats with their shoes on. He'd see high-school boys and girls, drinks from the vending machine on the table in front of them, fiddling with their phones, talking about friends who weren't there. He'd see junior-high girls, who had obviously not bought anything, sitting with their books spread out, preparing for tests. Takeru would watch them all vaguely, and then the old woman would arrive.

"Here she is," the junior-high girls would whisper to each other, snickering over their textbooks.

Takeru vaguely supposed they said the same sort of thing when he arrived: Here he comes! The boy in the cap. Look at him! He's still wearing that same Pokemon T-shirt in the middle of winter! And he still stinks of sweat!

The old woman was tiny, her back bent over double. She always wore a drab shirt and trousers, and was always pushing her shopping cart. To Takeru the bag in the cart looked like a little suitcase. She'd put the cart beside a table and sit down. Whenever someone came to sit nearby she'd stand up and try to push the cart closer to the table. "Sorry," she'd say. "In the way." As far as Takeru could see, there was plenty of space between the tables for people to get by, but despite what was obviously serious pain in her back, she always got up and tried to move the tightly packed cart. (In reality she didn't move it at all.) "Sorry. In the way." It was as if she were talking about herself. For Takeru there was something a little uncomfortable about her words, something unsettling. Was it because she was giving ground she didn't need to? Yet at the same time, and more powerfully, Takeru felt as though he was floating on something very soft, wrapped in a deep sense of relief. At times like this it seemed almost as if he had been forgiven. Being near the old woman must have made him feel that way, watching her give people space she didn't have to. But it's odd: unsettled and relieved—completely opposite emotions caused by exactly the same thing. Takeru probably no longer had the strength to think things through.

He liked watching the old woman put her hand slowly inside the cart to pull out a small white plastic bag. She'd take some *manju* or *mochi* from the bag that she'd bought at the store. Takeru enjoyed watching her slowly chew and swallow. He liked swinging his legs and waiting, wondering when she would finish. All he could have wanted was to watch from the side. He couldn't have been after anything more.

But one day their eyes met.

The old woman was about to eat a piece of mochi, but she returned it to its plastic container. She picked up another piece in her thin, veined hand and held it out to Takeru.

"Want one?" she asked.

He finished it before realizing he'd even started. He had no clear recollection of having eaten it at all. Suddenly he was worried that he hadn't thanked her.

"Thank you," he said.

"That's okay!"

Later, the old woman's voice would blend with Bunji's. It would never be drowned out. The two voices would become one. So perhaps even then, in the voice of the old woman, Takeru was hearing Bunji.

It's okay!

It's okay! Bunji's voice was already saying that all the time, even when the words seemed negative on their surface: *Don't! Don't! You mustn't!*

The voice affirmed everything about Takeru. Although it had no basis whatsoever for doing so, it accepted everything about him. This unsettled him, frightened him.

Takeru stared at the old woman. Her wrinkled face looked as though it could either be smiling or crying. Takeru decided to think she was always smiling.

He never went to the seating area in the supermarket with the intention of getting fed, but from then on the old woman always shared her snacks with him. And every time he thanked her, she'd say:

"That's okay!"

Takeru knew it wouldn't last long. He'd known ever since he first saw her. Didn't she keep saying, "In the way. Sorry," in that quiet voice, always worried that her shopping cart was an obstruction? She wasn't just talking about her cart—she was talking about herself. So, although she said, "That's okay" to Takeru, she would obstinately refuse to accept the same thing being said to her. That's why she had to speak in such a quiet voice— so nobody would respond with tolerance or forgiveness, so that when she said, "Sorry. In the way," nobody would reply, "That's okay." And nobody ever did.

When people looked at her bent, shuffling figure there was always a shade of irritation or embarrassment in their eyes. The old woman had forgiven Takeru, but there was no forgiveness for her. It seemed forbidden— forbidden both by her and by something else as well. It was as if, in order to forgive someone, she'd had to for- feit, in equal measure, the opportunity of being forgiven herself. But is the world where humans live so petty? The world—full of what Takeru only knew as the big thing—can it be so mean as to think a bent, wrinkled old woman, unsteady on her feet, is in the way? It can't be. But if it isn't, that means the old woman wished it upon herself, that her "In the way. Sorry" was a curse she used to punish herself. But even if that were the case, what had she done that had to be punished?

No. It couldn't be a punishment simply for sharing her manju with Takeru.

In Takeru's vague, unreliable memory it was the last day he ever saw the old woman. She gave him a treat as always—a manju, but then she bent forward over her cart, brought out another plastic container, and put it on the table. Inside were two more manju.

Her thin swollen-jointed fingers pushed the container gently toward Takeru. Then he heard her voice:

"Eat these with your little brother."

Did Takeru's trembling voice say, "Thank you"? And did he hear her all-forgiving voice reply:

"That's okay."

It's okay. Take it. Take it.

Did Bunji, of whose existence Takeru could have had no knowledge yet, shout that in a whisper (if that's possible) into his ear?

But was what she'd done something to be punished? Did she have to be punished for assuming Takeru was the older brother, for thinking of him and his older brother (yes, his brother was older, not younger), for wanting to share treats with them?

How, since Takeru had always been alone when they met, always completely alone, had the old woman known about his older brother (yes, his older brother, not younger)?

Who or what had told her? The big thing? That big thing that had told Joel about them? In which case, had Joel disappeared because he too had thought Takeru was the older brother? But the big thing, that great big thing— too big to be imagined—couldn't be so small-minded as to punish someone for a mistake over who was older, who was younger. His brother was older, Takeru was younger—a tiny fact like that couldn't bother the big thing, the colossal thing that embraced everything, accepted everything. So why the punishment? Punishment for what? Takeru tried to think, but he couldn't. It was like trying to draw water from a well with a broken bucket. The bucket always came up dry. Was the well so deep that all the water had seeped out by the time it reached his hands? Or was the well just empty? What was it that the big thing had punished? Who had been punished? His brother? No. Definitely not. Takeru? Me? But it wasn't Takeru who disappeared. Takeru was here. He was here, whether he liked it or not. The old woman disappeared and Joel disappeared. No. It wasn't just the old woman and Joel who disappeared.

His mother?

Takeru shook his head sharply to drive the thought away. Pointless notions bubbled and spat in his mind like wet things in a fire, they swarmed like flies around a dead fish. Frantically, he shook his head again. It was a stupid thing to do. That's what made his mother's face fall from the basket of his memory, never to be recovered.

His brother?

No. No. No.

Then (but when?) he heard. Two junior-high girls were chattering at the table next to his in the supermarket.

"He's not there!" said the thin one who had short hair and a face rather like an alpaca's. "When we arrived they said they weren't doing dolphin shows anymore. I thought, 'Oh no!'"

Takeru's heart pounded. Maybe he already knew what they were talking about.

"That's too bad," said her friend, owl-like in her glasses. "You've wanted to see him forever, haven't you? The supernatural dolphin!"

She burst out laughing.

"I like *so* wanted to see him!" said the alpaca, her voice getting louder. "But he's gone. It's, like, a real shame!"

They turned, astonished, to look at the boy who was suddenly standing right next to them and staring intently.

"Is that true? Really true?" asked Takeru.

"What's he want?" said the owl, pouting.

"What's wrong?" asked the alpaca.

"He's not there anymore?" said Takeru. "Johnnie's not there?"

"Huh? Johnnie? What's he talking about?" said the owl. She screwed up her nose in disgust, then suddenly laughed. "Johnnie? Who's that?"

"You mean the dolphin?" said the alpaca. "Right?"

"He's not there anymore? Johnnie's not there?"

"Ugh!" said the owl. "What're you crying for? Yuck!"

"Shut up! He's upset," said the alpaca.

"Yeah," she said, turning to Takeru. "He's gone."

Takeru was crying so hard he couldn't form any words. He pulled his Man U cap down to hide his eyes.

The tears didn't stop, but eventually he managed to speak. "Why? Why? Is he dead?"

It was as though he was asking himself as much as the girls. His voice trembled. The words seemed to disintegrate the moment they touched the air.

"I wish *you* were dead!" said the owl. "Go away!"

The alpaca, though, was doing her best to cheer Takeru up. Maybe she just wanted him to stop crying because he was attracting attention.

She kept talking, saying whatever came to mind.

"I don't know what happened to him, but they say he's not there anymore. I'm sure he's okay, though. Yeah, sure. I mean, like, nobody said he was dead. But he's gone. That's for sure. So…yeah, I guess maybe he escaped. He's, like, gone back to the sea. He's a dolphin after all. He'll be in the ocean somewhere, like, enjoying life. Yeah. Definitely."

While the alpaca rambled on the owl faced the other way, stifling her laughter.

But Takeru wasn't listening. He turned his back and, still crying, headed for the door. It was all too late.

Maybe there were some adults in the store who were worried about him, but with his cap pulled all the way down all he could see was the floor.

He came out of the supermarket and started running in despair. What pushed him now was the big thing. It didn't wrap him up and keep him warm, though. It didn't give him strength. It didn't affirm anything about him. Entirely the opposite. It had forsaken him. He was abandoned. Repulsed by the big thing, swept forward by overwhelming force, he could do nothing but run. Rejected, displaced, he had no choice but to go somewhere else, somewhere that wasn't here.

✽

The harsh din of cicadas filled the air. Earlier in the morning there would have been birdsong, playing along with the first rays of sunlight that crept down the western hill toward the village. The hillside would have shimmered in its gentle touch, before the rough assault of full light began. But now, all that could be heard were the cicadas. The newly formed shadows of all the things in the village quivered with their cries. The sound was like that of heavy rain, but the sky was clear. There was no mist out there, it was all in his head, among his memories. He was still in a daze, as always, and thoughts would not form properly. Takeru was sitting on Mitsuko's wooden veranda, taking large bites from a watermelon she'd cut for him.

He'd been out to the holly tree at the edge of the garden to shout for Saki to come and have some, but there'd been no reply.

"Looks like she's still asleep, Mitsuko," Takeru said as Mitsuko washed the dishes from breakfast in the kitchen.

"She shouldn't be lyin' 'round in bed, just 'cause it's the holidays," said Mitsuko, showing a hint of anger at

Saki's father, Tatsuya.

From Mitsuko's veranda you could see the hills around the village to the south. The blue sky above them was clear and bright. Takeru knew that the Pacific Ocean lay beyond the hills, and he imagined the sparkling sea. There was a beach over there where sea turtles came to lay their eggs. He wanted to see that.

"I'll take ya," Hii-chan had said. They were on the way back from shopping in town and had stopped for some gas at the Shudo Gas Station.

"But, Hii-chan," said Toshi, "they've only just laid their eggs."

"What difference does that make?" said Hii-chan, flaring his nostrils, making his nose look bigger than ever.

"Well, it's too late for Takeru. They won't be back 'til next summer, will they?" said Toshi, mockingly.

"He can stay 'til then," said Hii-chan smiling. His silver tooth glinted. "Suits ya here, don't it, Takeru? You've gotten fatter."

Hii-chan prodded Takeru's cheek. Takeru didn't know if he was fatter or not. Perhaps he was.

"You stay here long as ya like," said Hii-chan. "It'll be 'kay."

Okay. Okay. Takeru heard Bunji's voice too. He couldn't say where it came from.

Takeru tried to imagine himself staying here until the turtles came back to lay their eggs again. He couldn't really picture it. But despite that…no, probably because of it, he felt he'd be happy enough staying.

It was the day before their trip to Dolphin Village. They'd originally planned to go sooner, but there had been a series of early typhoons and the road along the coast had been closed because of a landslide.

Takeru heard the sound of a door slamming from across the field. He looked up. Saki was walking sleepily along the path, rubbing her eyes.

"Mornin'!" she shouted. "Did ya yell for me?"

"Yes! We've got some watermelon. Hurry up!"

Saki joined Takeru on the veranda and polished off two pieces of the watermelon. Then, without any partic-ular plan, they decided to go out.

"It's hot, Saki," said Mitsuko as they were leaving. "You'll have t'wear a hat, like Takeru."

"'kay."

"Look—here's the one ya left behind yesterday," Mitsuko said.

It was a straw hat with a ribbon. She placed it on Saki's head.

"You should be careful not t'forget things."

"Sorry! Thank ya."

Takeru had decided they should go to the temple first.

"What? Again?" said Saki.

"Why not?" Takeru said, walking quickly ahead.

The garden in front of the main building of the temple was entirely free of weeds and meticulously swept. The

black earth bore the neat lines of a bamboo rake, de-
terring deviation from the pathway. The noise of the cicadas was so unrelenting it could almost be ignored. It was
like a curtain of sound on top of which the birds drew
clear patterns of song. The humid air clung to Takeru's
body like an extra layer of skin. He felt as if he could have
pinched it between his fingers and pulled it away.

He couldn't remember his mother's face; but he
remembered the old woman in the supermarket in
Akeroma—her skin, brown-stained and loose, as though
hanging directly off her bones.

The sticky, clinging air protected Takeru from
reality. Or distanced him from it. Perhaps those are the
same thing in the end.

Okay. Okay.

Bunji wasn't visible through the thick film of heat
shimmering in the air.

Takeru looked up. A thin white trail of clouds pre-
vented the blue of the sky from penetrating his eyes.
Bare blue sky frightened him, as if his mind might be
sucked into its depths.

The birds sang louder, and for a moment the mem-
brane of heat seemed about to burst. The surface of the
air rose and fell, as though it were breathing. But the
world was with Takeru like it always was, or perhaps it
was showing a calmer, friendlier face than normal. The
light, softened by white clouds, was smiling down on
everything that remained in the world. All things had

been accepted. Did his mother hate this scenery in spite of this? Did she want to get away as soon as possible, in spite of this? He heard kittens mewing somewhere. The somewhere was within him—as if he were a bag and the kittens were closed up inside. But that didn't trouble him. He felt good, and not just from running up the stone steps. Everything was forgiven. He may or may not have formed that thought in words. But what enveloped him—the clinging heat; the peaceful-looking sky; the soft light; the birdsong—it expanded his being, generous and wide. Takeru's mind normally shrank when he thought of his mother and brother—the kittens in the tightly sealed bag crying for help, cries that might never leave his ears—but now his mind was growing, swelling out, so that, though still heartrending, the kittens' cries were now further off. But they were still inside, there was no difference there. What am I thinking? What have the kittens done to be tied up in a bag? What have I done? Tell me. Tell me.

"What're you doin', Takeru?"

Saki had been walking up the path to the graveyard behind the temple, but had retraced her steps to where Takeru was standing in front of the main building, his palms pressed together in front of his face.

"Praying," replied Takeru.

"Look up there!" said Saki, her voice suddenly loud.

She was pointing up the hill. Takeru could see nothing special among the rows of graves.

"Not there. Farther up! Look!"

Takeru looked higher. On the boundary between the graveyard and the woods beyond was a small figure sitting on a large branch in a tree. It was hunched over like an old woman.

Takeru immediately looked away.

"Bunji?" he murmured. What made him think that?

"What'd you say?" asked Saki, her voice low now too.

"Nothing… It's a monkey," he said, putting into words what his eyes saw.

"Yeah," said Saki, looking at the ground. "Make sure you don't catch its eye."

Takeru looked down too. He reacted more to the fear in her breath than the words themselves. If you catch a monkey's eye it might bite you.

"It's drunk," he said.

It seemed funny once he'd said it. All Japanese monkeys have red faces, but according to Hii-chan's personal theory of evolution the red faces of the monkeys here came from drinking the liquor that people left at their loved ones' graves.

Saki tried to nod, but her chin was already against her chest. All they had to do was avoid the monkey's gaze, but the children were so nervous that their eyes were glued to the ground and they didn't even look at each other. Then, as though prearranged, they simultaneously turned their heads. They tried to make the movement look casual, as if they were tracking some troublesome mosquito. Once their heads were turned, they rotated their bodies as well until they had their backs to the graveyard, and to the monkey beyond it.

The path they were standing on had been cemented by the head priest, an avid do-it-yourselfer. Older villagers on their daily visits to the graveyard did not let themselves be deterred by wet concrete, so the path, far from smooth anyway, was peppered with footprints. Hii-chan had mentioned that there were also prints left by deer and boar. Takeru wondered if Bunji's footprints might be there too. He scoured the surface. "What kind of footprints are those?" he said, pointing. "A monkey's," laughed Saki, not bothering to take a closer look. There were piles of weeds on the side of the path, pulled up by the old folks visiting the graves. In some places the weeds had been snapped off, rather than pulled up completely. They'd soon grow again, their leaves spreading and waving in the wind. Perhaps the old folks left the roots in so they could have a reason to come back more often.

From the graveyard there was quite a clear view of the head priest's house, only partially obstructed by a clump of bamboo grass. They could see the priest's daughter-in-law hanging out laundry in the garden. On one pole was a sheet billowing gently in the wind. On another were pieces of toweling.

"What are those?" asked Takeru.

"Diapers, of course," said Saki, like she was amazed by his ignorance.

"Oh."

"Cloth diapers like those're a real luxury. There's so much laundry t'do."

"Oh."

Takeru remembered that his brother had worn disposable diapers for a long time. It had been odd having his older brother wear diapers when he himself no longer had to.

"Paper must be easier," he said.

"Cloth's better for the environment," said Saki.

"Oh. Still, it must be a real pain doing all that laundry," he said.

But wearing the same clothes every day or not taking a bath didn't kill people. Takeru thought of his time in Akeroma. One morning when it was cold and the days were short, Joel came to visit them. He brought his few household items and gave them to Takeru, along with a folded ten-thousand-yen note. The blankets had a spicy smell. After that, every time he thought of Joel that smell came back to him. Joel told him he was going home for Christmas, and that he might not be able to come back to Japan. There was sadness in his large eyes. Takeru wondered how Joel knew he might not be able to come back, so he asked. Joel replied, in his slow, stumbling Japanese. He seemed to be saying that if he left Japan he might not be allowed back in. He used words like "permit" and "visa," which Takeru didn't understand, even in Japanese. Unless someone was dead, why would they be unable to come back? Takeru was already in the village by the sea when he heard about the big earthquake that had happened early in the New Year. The name of the country seemed familiar, and although it had been over six months since the disaster happened, Mitsuko found an article for him about it in an old newspaper. The Chinese characters in the article were too complex for Takeru to understand everything, but the map looked familiar and he got that over three hundred thousand people had been killed. The number was beyond Takeru's imagination. Was that the country Joel came from? He wasn't sure. For all Takeru knew, Joel might be back in Akeroma by now, worried that Takeru and his brother weren't there or, perhaps, relieved they weren't.

A strong gust of wind blew down the hill, dispersing the smell of Joel and lifting the sheet on the laundry pole. The sheet gave a flapping sound like the wings of a large bird, though its movement was more like the squirm of someone concealing something under their coat. The young woman was busy hanging out more laundry. Neither Takeru nor Saki could take their eyes off of her and the baby on her back. Takeru began to feel hot at the back of his neck. Perhaps it was sunlight filtering through the mass of leaves, or perhaps it was the gaze of the monkey in the tree. The baby started to cry. The mother left the laundry for a moment and turned around.

The baby stopped crying.

The mother didn't seem to see Takeru and Saki. If Takeru felt the power of the monkey's gaze behind him, why couldn't the mother notice his own burning stare?

It was the baby. That's why she didn't notice. The baby could feel his gaze, but it wasn't crying yet. Takeru stared harder.

It began to fidget.

That's it! Be miserable!

Don't! Don't do that!

But Takeru didn't listen. He knew that whatever Bunji said, even if it sounded negative, was an affirmation of everything about him.

The baby bawled. But time was running faster now, and so the mother's reaction was fast too. She'd already turned away from the laundry pole.

Perhaps that's what Takeru had wanted to see her do. Perhaps that's why he'd put so much effort into his stare.

The mother turned around. But not, of course, to meet Takeru's gaze.

The baby wasn't going to share its mother with anybody. It monopolized the mother's attention and entirely negated anybody else who might be staring at her longingly. It was as though Takeru had been staring at the baby, trying to make it miserable, because he had wanted to see the mother's emotion channeled toward it, her love bound to it.

It made Takeru want to cry. But no, maybe his sadness came just from seeing the baby's impotence—though it cried with all its might, its whole body convulsing, it was, in this vast world, entirely helpless. But Takeru was helpless too. Perhaps he was sad because the baby's crying made him realize just how helpless and alone he was.

"Sounds healthy, don't it?" Saki said.

Her voice brought Takeru back to earth.

"It's doing its job...crying," he said.

"It's so cute!" said Saki, though she couldn't see the baby's face.

"Babies have one other job too," said Takeru. "Do you know what that is?"

"No," said Saki.

"Don't just say no... Think!"

Saki crossed her arms and cocked her head. A mischievous look came to her eye.

"Poopin'."

"Bull's-eye!" said Takeru, laughing loudly.

"Shh," said Saki, putting her finger to her lips, "she'll notice us."

But the woman seemed conscious only of her crying baby—all other sounds were blocked out entirely. She cradled it in her arms, not looking up the hill once. *Yo-i yoi, yo-i yoi*, she chanted, swaying the child from side to side. The cry seemed out of keeping with her youthful appearance, her neat, dyed-brown hair. It sounded like an old person's. But why?

The newly washed sheet must have been heavy, but it moved easily in the wind, as though the sun had already dried it out. It rose and fell like a wave, and with it the mother's loving voice bobbed gently up and down: *Yo-i yoi, yo-i yoi.* The baby's crying gradually faded away, breaking up like smoke in the wind. Takeru's body shook, tickled by rising laughter. He inhaled deeply, and as the smell of grass and leaves flowed through his nose to his chest, he no longer felt the helplessness of a baby. *Yo-i yoi, yo-i yoi.*

The hill of the graveyard behind the temple was not that high, but the view extended over the head priest's residence to the houses beyond. Windows and roofs glared with reflected sunlight. The telephone wires linking the houses swayed from time to time, shaking off birds and the clinging air. Farther away was the sea. The sea and the sky slumbered like twin beasts, their breath, heat, and bodies kneaded inseparably together. Time too lay still. Takeru had a strange feeling that he wasn't here. No, Takeru *was* here. He was here, but it seemed as if "here" was inside someone else's memory. *Yo-i yoi, yo-i yoi.* The mother's tender, gentle, soothing voice wrapped around him, lifting him up from a place higher and further than the light of the sun, and taking him away. If Takeru were inside someone else's dream, that person hadn't noticed him. The clear sunlight played with the shining tiles. It squabbled with the shadows, jostling to be the confidant of the green leaves and grass that quivered and whispered in the wind. But Takeru was not noticed. He wanted to lift his hand and wave.

Because he feels uneasy being forgotten? Is that why he wants to wave? No, that doesn't frighten him at all. But doesn't he feel uneasy waving, when this isn't his place? He doesn't know. But he wants to communicate that he is here. He simply wants to declare the fact that he is filled by something big, strong, and positive. Hey!… Hey!

But then he heard a voice.

There was something like hatred in it. And it shot him out of the sky. Irrespective of whether this was his place or not, his mind had been expanding to cover the entire world. But the voice stopped that.

Takeru turned around. The monkey in the tree was beaming, laughing, its canines jutting from its ecstatic mouth, its bright red face strangely contorted. Perhaps it had been into the liquor on the graves. Takeru immediately turned his back. He stumbled and almost fell. Was he drunk from the monkey's stare?

Takeru was laughing. Laughing, sounding happy. And it wasn't just Takeru and the monkey—the laughter in the air was so loud and boisterous it was as if all the dead in the graveyard might have been laughing too. It whirled around inside his head. He could hear nothing else. He could not hear the cicadas. Where were the mewing kittens? Was the baby crying? The flapping of the sheets and diapers in the wind…he couldn't hear them either. No, he could. He could hear all sounds. And so he could hear nothing. He could think about nothing.

There was the sound of chafing blades of grass. *I hated it, detested it. I wanted to get away as soon as I could.* The pressure on his back suddenly lightened, and he turned his head. There was no sign now of the monkey on the branch. The drunken animal must have fallen from the tree and gone back to its home in the hills.

That afternoon Takeru was watching high-school base-ball on TV with Mitsuko when he heard Hii-chan's truck pull up behind the house.

"Octopus!" cried Hii-chan, coming into the garden with a net bag.

Mitsuko immediately stood and went outside.

"It's huge!" she said.

"They caught it in a pot this mornin', and it's been in a tank by the quay all day. They brought it out just now and gave it t'me."

Takeru joined them outside. They were standing by the washtub, looking down at the soft mass of red and black that had slipped from the net bag. Takeru prod-ded the slimy body nervously with his finger. The color changed slightly where he touched it. It was beautiful. But Takeru said, "Ugh! It's disgusting!"

"It may look disgustin', but it'll taste good," said Mitsuko happily. "And it's so big!"

"Boil it over charcoal—it'll be wonderful," Hii-chan said.

"Yeah, yeah," said Mitsuko, retrieving the charcoal grill from the storage space.

She asked Hii-chan to light the grill and went into the kitchen, bringing out a large tin bowl and a box of salt. The octopus clung to her hands as she lifted it from the tub. She crouched down, put it into the bowl on the ground, poured a vast quantity of salt on it, and rubbed it vigorously.

"Do you always use so much?" asked Takeru.

"You'll never get the slime off otherwise," she said.

She squeezed her fingers tight as she pulled the octopus through her hand. From time to time she lifted it and then brought it down hard against the bottom of the bowl. The octopus was now covered in thick white bubbles—a mixture of salt and slime. For some reason Takeru thought of his brother. It was strange that nobody ever asked about him. Mitsuko pressed her fingers hard into the inside of the octopus's head and pushed it inside out.

"Ugh!" cried Takeru.

He shuddered at the different shapes and colors of the octopus's guts. Mitsuko scraped them away, throwing them nonchalantly into the sink.

"Water's ready," said Hii-chan, a fan in one hand. A large gold-colored tin pot was bubbling away over the grill.

"Well," said Hii-chan. "I done my bit, so I'll be off t'home now." He smiled at Takeru. "Enjoy it!"

"We'll bring some over when it's ready," said Mitsuko.

"Don't bother. I had some the other day. Eat it all yourselves."

He walked to his truck and waved.

Mitsuko took the lid off the pot and slipped the octopus into the seething water.

"Oh, I forgot somethin'," she said, then disappeared into the kitchen. She came back with some tea leaves and vinegar and put them into the boiling water. "That'll help soften the octopus," she said.

"Mitsuko?" said Takeru.

"Yes?"

"In that photo on the altar there's that child named Bunji, right?"

"Bunji? Oh yeah, Bunji."

"You said he died when he was small. Are you sure?"

Mitsuko's face flickered with surprise. She looked at him, as though trying to figure him out.

"Why're you askin' 'bout that again?"

Takeru hesitated. He couldn't bring himself to say it: *I know him; I've seen him; I'm always hearing his voice.* He couldn't say that. Instead his mouth said:

"How did he die? Was he sick?"

"I may've said he died when he was little, but I suppose he was 'bout twelve or thirteen. It was before I was born, so I don't know that much 'bout him, but they say he was a bit weak—not just his body, his head too. He didn't go t'school—he couldn't. These days there're schools for people like that, but not back then. But havin' him wanderin' around the village wasn't no nuisance to people. I suppose they just accepted it. One day, though, he went away somewhere."

"Went away somewhere? You mean he disappeared?"

"Yeah," said Mitsuko, lifting the lid of the pot to check on the octopus.

"Where?"

"Nobody knew. Night came and he didn't come home. The whole village was worried 'bout him. In those days when someone disappeared people thought they'd been taken by spirits. If it happened in the mountains, they'd blame *tengu*; if it was at sea, they'd blame sea spirits. It was that long ago. Anyway, the last place Bunji was seen was Lion Cross Point. A fisherman was comin' back t'shore in his boat when he looked over to the point and saw him and another child of 'bout the same height... People thought the other one must've been Takeshi, his younger brother—the one we all thought ya were named after. He was a kind and clever boy. He always was lookin' after Bunji—like Takeshi was the older brother and Bunji the younger one. From what the fisherman said it sounded like Takeshi was leadin' Bunji by the hand. Everybody asked Takeshi, but he said he didn't know anythin' 'bout it, that he never went as far as Lion Cross Point. Well, Takeshi wasn't the type of child to tell lies, so in the end everybody came 'round to thinkin' Bunji had drowned. So, though I said he died, nobody had any real proof. There wasn't a body, so they couldn't be sure he was dead. And we can't ask Takeshi again now—he's not with us anymore either. I expect they're together in Heaven, walkin' along hand in hand, just like they did here."

"Mitsuko," said Takeru. Or perhaps he didn't.

Takeshi was lying, he wanted to say. He *was* with Bunji. I know he was.

Because Takeru saw them. He didn't know whether they were at Lion Cross Point, but he saw Takeshi and Bunji walking together. Takeshi went ahead and Bunji tried to keep up with him. Takeshi looked irritated, as though Bunji were a nuisance. Bunji walked at Takeshi's heels, keeping as close as he could. His elbows were bent, and he looked off-balance, as though he might fall over or walk into the middle of the road at any moment. There wouldn't have been any cars here in those days. The road wouldn't have been paved. But Takeru saw the odd car go by, sometimes a truck or bus.

Strangely, they were both wearing caps. Takeshi's was a Man U cap, and Bunji's—FC Barcelona. But maybe it wasn't so strange after all—both clubs are over a hundred years old. Where were the boys going? They kept on walking. Even farther? Even farther. The older one needed to pee—the younger one knew the signs. There was a large field beside the road. There was a notice that said "For Sale." Were there any broad open spaces like that near the village? Maybe there had been then—there would have been many fewer houses in those days. The younger one took down the older one's pants at the corner of the field. As soon as they were down, dark yellow pee spurted out from the tip of his swollen penis. It landed on the grass, and some splashed against Takeru's shin—not Takeru's...Takeshi's. The grass where the pee hit turned yellow, turned brown, turned black, as though it had been burned. It withered away almost instantly. No, just the opposite. It grew...furiously twining around the boys' feet. So they left. The older one's pants weren't all the way up, so his bottom was showing and people snickered as they passed. They could laugh. That was okay. They could mock. That was okay. But why didn't they stop them? The boys waited at the bus stop. After a while a bus came. *Do you go to the aquarium?* Takeshi asked the driver. So Takeshi wanted to go there too, thought Takeru. But was there an aquarium in those days? The village is by the sea. They don't have to go to an aquarium to see things—well maybe they couldn't see sea otters, but lobsters, crabs, octopuses, rays, even dolphins were just there. And what would be the point of going now? There are no dolphins at the aquarium anymore. Perhaps Takeshi didn't know. The dolphins weren't there, which meant the older brother couldn't swim with them, which meant he'd never get better. *Get on this bus to the terminal, then change to the 6 or the 21*, said the driver. Takeshi took a ten-thousand-yen note from his pocket to pay for the tickets. It was just like the one that Joel had given

MASATSUGU ONO

Takeru. Had Yukichi Fukuzawa's face been on the note for so long? Someone in the village said Fukuzawa came from their own Oita prefecture. But someone else said he came from the northern part and had nothing to do with the south. So there's no luck with money or work in the south, said another. The driver frowned at the bill. *Got nothin' smaller?* Then he looked at the older brother. *Don't worry about his fare*, he said. *Why? Just don't.* Was it because Bunji didn't go to school and so didn't qualify as a student for fares? *Don't worry about yours either*, said the driver. Was it because there was almost nobody on the bus? *It's okay. Just get on*, said the driver, giving a slow wink. *Just don't tell anyone.* Takeru didn't see much of them after that. The bus was comfortable and its vibrations made him sleepy. He was woken by the driver. His brother was asleep beside him. He shook him awake. They got off the bus hand in hand. He looked for the stop for the 6 or 21. A 21 bus had arrived. They got on. Again, the older one didn't have to pay. *Do you want to get on right now?* asked the driver. *I'm not leaving for a while.* It didn't matter. They sat down at the back of the bus. The heater was on. The windows were steamed up. The older one was already asleep. The younger one took his brother's FC Barcelona cap gently from his head. That was the one he'd really wanted, but he hadn't been able to say. He took off his own cap and put it on the older one's head. He put the older one's cap on his own head. Takeru looked at the window, but he didn't see his face reflected there with

111

the cap on his head. Was that because the window was steamed up? Was that the only reason? He felt dizzy. He felt sick. He looked at his brother, who was fast asleep with his head against the window, mouth half open. His breathing was awkward and saliva dribbled from his mouth. Leaving his brother asleep, Takeru stood up and asked the driver if there was a place where he could use the bathroom. Did he need to be sick? Did his stomach hurt? Did he just want to pee? There were a few other passengers on the bus now, sitting here and there. *The nearest public toilet is over there*, said the driver. *Hurry up. I'm leaving soon.* So Takeru ran from the bus to the bath-room. A cone blocked the entrance. The bathroom was being cleaned. He heard water from a hose washing down the floor. He rushed over to the shopping center across from the bus station. It was crowded. Everyone was laden with shopping bags, but they didn't block each other's way. Takeru's chest was blocked, though. He could hardly breathe. Where was the bathroom? He couldn't see one. He wanted to cry. He cried. He cried. He waited as his tears flowed, as time flowed quickly by. Was that what happened? He didn't know what he was doing. He knew. He didn't know anything. He knew everything. Had the bus carrying his brother arrived at Lion Cross Point?

"Takeru!"

The sound of Ken's voice made Takeru jump.

"Shocked t'see me?" said Ken, laughing.

"You off work already?" Mitsuko asked Ken.

"Finished 'bout three. I was washin' the company truck," said Ken. "But more interestin' than that—Ito Fisheries caught a dolphin in one of their nets."

"That's strange," Mitsuko said.

"Yeah, that's why I came over," said Ken. "Takeru, you want t'come and have a look? I can take ya."

"What?" asked Takeru, looking up at Ken. "Now? To see the dolphin they caught?"

"Yeah."

"But we're still going to Dolphin Village tomorrow, aren't we?"

"Yeah," Mitsuko intervened. "You'll see lots of dolphins tomorrow. There's no harm in not goin' today."

"Well...thing is, Mitsuko," said Ken awkwardly, "there was that storm the other day..."

"The one that blocked the road?"

"Yeah. That storm hit Dolphin Village. I found out yesterday from my friend who has that yellowtail farm o'er in Shishinome."

"Hit? You mean it was damaged?"

"Some huge waves came smashin' into the bay and ripped the nettin' of the dolphin pen. A lot of 'em escaped."

"The dolphins escaped?" exclaimed Takeru.

"That's what I heard. And now they're eating all the fish in the fishin' grounds. It's a real problem."

Mitsuko looked mystified.

"If it was such a big problem you'd think it'd been in the newspaper. I read it every day, but I ain't seen nothing 'bout that."

"Can't say," said Ken. "Don't look at the newspapers much. But that was what my friend told me. And I figure the one they caught must've been from Dolphin Village. That'd make sense."

"I wonder," said Mitsuko dubiously. "Just 'cause a dolphin's escaped doesn't mean it's gonna swim straight into a net. They're supposed to be clever, ain't they?"

"They can cure people," said Takeru.

Neither Mitsuko nor Ken was listening.

"Well, anyway, it's my day off tomorrow so I'll take Takeru and Saki to Dolphin Village, and if it's closed we'll go on a bit farther to the prefectural aquarium. It'll be quick on the highway and there's lots t'see there. That'd be 'kay, right Takeru?"

"Do they have dolphins?" asked Takeru.

"Course. And they've got otters and sea lions too. They have a dolphin show, and a sea lion show as well. That'll work, won't it?"

"Yes," said Takeru. "It's fine by me. But what about Saki?"

"If it's 'kay with you, I'm sure Saki won't mind," said Ken.

"Yeah," said Mitsuko. "It'll be good, Takeru. Just next to the aquarium there's a place where they feed wild monkeys. Get Ken to take ya there too."

"I think I've seen enough monkeys," said Takeru, looking slightly embarrassed. "There are lots around here."

"That's true," said Mitsuko, smiling.

"And we've got Hii-chan too," said Ken.

Takeru laughed as he pictured the old man's monkey-like features.

"Don't go sayin' things like that!" said Mitsuko, though she was laughing as well.

The next day Ken came to pick them up at 8:30 as promised. Saki had gotten up early and come over to Mitsuko's house at 7:00 for breakfast.

The children were ready in good time and sat waiting eagerly for Ken to arrive. There had been rain overnight, but it had stopped around dawn, and by the time they got into the car there were just a few dark clouds left in the sky to the east.

The village always stank of the sea. The stench of rotting shellfish hung heavy in the air, especially after rain. Driving around the bay, the smell of the sea never left your nostrils, even with the windows closed, and the road wound on endlessly, so Takeru had always felt carsick when he first arrived. But that didn't last long. You could get used to a smell even if you hated it. You could probably get used to a place too, Takeru thought, if you lived there long enough—even a place you hated, detested.

They turned right at the bus stop. Old Tsuru was

already sitting there, the spot already bathed in sunshine. Tsuru saw them and lifted his hand. But no. He wasn't acknowledging Takeru, Saki, or Ken, but something bigger. But now Takeru was inside that big thing, so why not say Tsuru was acknowledging him? Takeru guessed that in Tsuru's raised fist was his glass eye. Takeru didn't know if that eye would see, but he raised his own hand and gave a little wave in Tsuru's direction.

Takeru was looking out the window. There was nothing remarkable about the color of the sky or the shapes of the clouds. That sky could have been anywhere. He looked toward the hills beyond the bay. They were covered in trees. Birds, animals, and insects lived there, but he couldn't see them or sense them. The sea was a perfectly normal dark blue. Fish, crabs, and octopuses lived there, but he couldn't see them or sense them either. He saw the long quay floating on the bay. There were birds walking on it and flying above it—big herons and seedy-looking hawks with missing feathers. Sometimes they landed on the narrow shoulder of the coast road and lingered for a while. He looked at the shapes of people's houses, the colors of the roofs, and the sunlight they reflected. The narrow road. The slanting telephone poles. The black, sagging telephone wires. He was part of this landscape now, so his mother must also hate him.

The houses became fewer and farther between. The

road curved in and out along the coast from one village to the next. It was narrow and had no center line.

The speed limit was 30 kmph, but Ken knew the curves well and was driving at nearly 50 kmph. He drove very differently than Mitsuko. She always kept within the speed limit. If she saw a car coming up fast in the rearview mirror, she'd mutter: "Oh no, he's right behind me! I don't like that. Let's get rid of him." When she reached a suitable place, she'd pull over and let her exasperated followers (the people in both the driver and passenger seats were almost always acquaintances) go ahead. "What's the rush?" she'd say, sharing her mild irritation with Takeru. If a roadside mirror showed a car coming around the curve in the opposite direction, she'd break sharply, nearly stopping, to give the other car space to pass freely. She was very serious about driving safely, especially with a child in the car.

Ken's car, with Takeru and Saki in the back, drove on, curve after curve. Eventually, Lion Cross Point came into view, jutting sharply out into the sea toward the headland on the far side of the bay. The road followed the coast out toward the Point.

"I still don't know why it's called Lion Cross Point, Takeru," said Ken, "but let me tell ya 'bout something I do know that happened here once. You'll find it interestin', both of you."

"What?" asked Saki, leaning forward.

"It's 'bout your dad, Tatsuya, and Takeru's ma, Wakako."

Takeru had never heard any stories about his mother from when she was young. He listened nervously to what Ken said:

Tatsuya had just bought his first car. He'd left school and had begun working at Kawase Fisheries. He'd managed to save enough to buy a used Skyline R31. He wanted to take it out for a drive, so he asked Wakako to come with him. She was a year younger, in her third year at the local high school.

Takeru couldn't tell from what Ken was saying whether they had been boyfriend and girlfriend.

Tatsuya had suggested Ken come along with them in his own car (a used Civic), so Ken was following them. Ken was worried that Tatsuya was going a bit too fast—he was an inexperienced driver, taking the bends very wide. It was late ("Your mother wasn't the studyin' type," Ken said), so luckily there wasn't anyone coming in the opposite direction. Still, it was a dangerous way to drive. Ken's heart was in his mouth. He felt something was going to happen and then it did.

"What?" asked Saki eagerly.

Just then Takeru saw something.

"Look!" he said, pointing toward the sea beyond Lion Cross Point.

The water was shining like molten silver in the morning sun. Something had risen gently to the surface. The light behind it was dazzling, but there was no doubt about what it was.

Ken kept talking, though, his eyes on Lion Cross Point:

Tatsuya's car was approaching the Point. They started going around the curve. Ken's car followed. But suddenly, to Ken's astonishment, Tatsuya's car was no longer in front of him. It had disappeared entirely.

"Disappeared? What do ya mean, Ken?" said Saki.

Takeru gazed silently at what had appeared on the surface of the sea.

"It just disappeared," said Ken. "I couldn't understand it. A moment earlier it'd been right there in front of me. I thought it might've been carried away by spirits."

But it was nothing like that. The explanation was simple. The car hadn't made it around the bend. It was going too fast, couldn't manage the turn, and went crashing through the guardrail. ("No," he said on reflection, "I don't suppose there was a guardrail at Lion Cross Point in them days.") It dove straight into the sea.

"Dove? Splash?" laughed Saki.

Ken smiled.

"It's nothin' to laugh 'bout, Saki," he said. "Well, I can smile 'bout it now, too, but it was terrifyin'. There were no lights on the road, and it was completely dark. They could easily have drowned. I could hear the car sinkin'. I turned my car so the headlights were shinin' over the water. There were bubbles comin' up to the surface. *They're dead*, I thought. I really did."

"But they weren't dead, were they?" Saki said. "Thank goodness!"

"They were lucky. It was late summer and still hot, so the car windows were all open.

"They'd both been brought up by the sea, so they were good swimmers. They managed t'climb out the windows and swim up. I was so relieved when I saw their heads bobbin' on the surface. I had been 'bout to dive in myself."

Takeru tried to imagine it. What had his mother seen? Was that what made her hate this place, detest it? Was that why she'd wanted to get away as soon as she could? Takeru could see something. Might this be what his mother saw? As she struggles to get out the window of the sinking car, from the dark depths of the silent ocean, a dolphin suddenly appears, its body swaying through the water. It swims up close. Its eyes meet hers. It puts its pointed mouth to her ear. She sees the neat lines of its teeth. It whispers. It whispers gently. It tells her important things—about her future, about the two brothers, about what will happen and what can't be avoided. His mother nods. She nods. But does she understand? Does she really comprehend? The dolphin turns. It encourages her and she doesn't hesitate. She could have, perhaps she should have, but instead she stretches out her hand and grips the fin on the dolphin's back. It flicks its tail and heads straight up to the surface, bringing her back to the world.

But was that a good thing?

It's okay, it's okay, said a voice—a reply from what had surfaced beyond Lion Cross Point, trying to erase Takeru's doubts, doubts that would never disappear.